GETTING OLD CAN HURT YOU

GETTING OLD CAN HURT YOU

Rita Lakin

Severn House Large Print
London & New York

This first large print edition published 2019
in Great Britain and the USA by
SEVERN HOUSE PUBLISHERS LTD of
Eardley House, 4 Uxbridge Street, London W8 7SY.
First world regular print edition published 2018 by
Severn House Publishers Ltd.

British Library Cataloguing in Publication Data
A CIP catalogue record for this title is available from the British Library.

ISBN-13: 9780727829689

Severn House Publishers support the Forest Stewardship Council™
[FSC™], the leading international forest certification organisation. All
our titles that are printed on FSC certified paper carry the FSC logo.

Typeset by Palimpsest Book Production Ltd.,
Falkirk, Stirlingshire, Scotland.
Printed and bound in Great Britain by
T J International, Padstow, Cornwall.

To my sons, Howard and Gavin,
the best sons any mother could want

Introduction to our Characters

GLADDY & HER GLADIATORS:

Gladys (Gladdy) Gold 75   Our heroine and her funny, adorable and sometimes impossible partners. Married to Jack

Evelyn (Evvie) Markowitz 73   Gladdy's sister. Logical, a regular Sherlock Holmes, now remarried to Joe

Ida Franz 71   Stubborn, mean, great for in-your-face confrontation

Bella Fox 83   The 'shadow' she's so forgettable, she's perfect for surveillance, but smarter than you think

Sophie Meyerbeer 79   She lives for color-coordination

YENTAS, KIBITZERS, SUFFERERS: THE INHABITANTS OF PHASE TWO

Hy Binder 75   A man of a thousand tasteless jokes

Lola Binder 74   Hy's wife who hasn't a
thought in her head that he hasn't put there

Tessie Hoffman   66   Chubby, loves to gossip,
married to:

Sol Spankowitz 75   married to Tessie

THE COP AND THE COP'S POP

Morgan (Morrie) Langford 40   Tall, lanky,
sweet and smart

Jack Langford 75   Handsome and romantic,
married to Gladdy

AND: MAIN CHARACTERS THIS STORY

Tori   Ida's granddaughter
Marilyn and Shirley   her sisters
Fred and Helen   Tori's parents
Max and Gertrude   Tori's other grandparents
Izzy Dix   former crook
Chaz Dix

Part One
The Arrival

Prologue
The Deli

My girls and I are enjoying a yearly celebration lunch of our favorite Private Eye cases, at our usual deli, The Continental. The Dr Brown's cream soda is flowing freely and the congratulatory high-fives keep going around. In between bites of cheese blintzes, of course.

The long-established Fort Lauderdale restaurant is crowded with huge groups – there's always some Hadassah-type organization events, also birthdays and anniversaries, as well as the hungry mobs from the various neighborhood retirement homes.

But we girls are well-known customers and a table is always available for us.

Sophie, color-coordinated, a vision in pink – pink pedal pushers, pink shorts, pink hair – clinks her glass in toast with all the others. The sound is accompanied by the music made by her many clunky bracelets. 'My vote for favorite case is when we read about the woman who hit a purse-snatcher guy with her cane, and within weeks, Cane Fu classes were opened. We got to use canes to capture a murderer.'

Bella, our often-puzzled partner, wears a typical dove gray pant suit, lavender blouse, headband and flip-flops, giggles, 'I liked the squirrels who robbed the car wash. But I never figured out how they spent the money.'

My sister, Evvie, in yellow sweats and matching sneakers, raises her glass next. 'To Grandpa Bandit, my favorite crook!'

I, in my conventional beige tee and skirt, smile at the girls traveling down memory lane. I'm Gladdy Gold, reluctant appointed leader of the pack, and I gaze contentedly at my charges. Sure we are in our seventies and eighties, but we'll remain 'girls' to the end. We know we're all in the checkout line for the big deli in the sky, but until then we are totally involved in the Gladdy Gold detective agency. Our motto, 'Never Trust Anyone Under Seventy-Five'. Senior Sleuths to the Senior Citizen. Our slogan – 'We Take Care of Our Own'.

Bella, our oldest at eighty-three, looks perplexed at Evvie's comment, bleary blue eyes squinting, pursing her lips whenever bewildered. It's slowly dawning on her. 'But we let Grandpa Bandit get away.'

Ida, who is known for her impatience and the tightness of her battleship-gray hair bun, barks at her. 'Yes, but the cops caught him and he did his time!'

'We're so smart,' Bella says, nodding cheerfully. She takes another sip of her cream soda.

Evvie pokes Ida. 'Remember when he sent us those letters with the little green feathers enclosed?'

Ida pokes her in return. 'Introducing himself as Robin Hood, who stole from the young to pay for the old and poor who needed surgery!'

'I can't believe he's dumb enough to come back here, now that he has a record.' Sophie slurps at her lemonade. She doesn't like cream soda.

'Because,' I say, waving the letter we received today, 'he had liked it so much while he was doing his robbing jobs, and met such nice people like us, he decided he'd retire here. And he's invited us over to his home for tea.'

Evvie is amused. 'So Izzy now lives in a house, four blocks away from our police station. That's so funny.'

Bella claps her hands in delight. 'Is he? Is he who?'

Ida sighs. We've been down this path before. 'Here we go again. Izzy is his name.'

Bella is still perplexed, but game to be included, anyway. 'That's so sweet. Is he Izzy, Is Izzy is his name? Whoever Izzy is, tee-hee, he invited us over for tea. Should we go? I never visited a convict's house. Do we wear striped dresses? Will he steal our purses?'

Ida is about to hit her for her idiocy, but a look from me stops her. Besides, there is something happening at the front door.

We all turn to check the action. Erwin, the deli manager, is holding onto a scruffy-looking teenager, his voice sharp, his fingertips barely grabbing onto her shoulder, not wanting to touch this unsanitary creature. This is surprising behavior for that sweetly, benign soul who never raises his voice. Ever. 'You can't come in like this. You have to wear shoes!' he shouts in frustration.

Fifty pairs of eyes lift from the deli delight of their choice. They glance over at Erwin's detainee

5

and travel down to the girl's noticeably dirty, unshod feet. Then look upward to the wild hazel eyes and filthy tangled brown hair, and move down again to obviously unwashed jeans. 'My-oh-mys' and 'Tut-tuts' all over the room.

'Hey! Let go, nerd!' The girl shouts at Erwin. 'I have to see my grandmother. I know she's here!'

Erwin is a merciless manager, follower of many rules. 'I don't care if you want to see Tinker Bell. You are not coming in!'

The teenager cries out again, yelling. 'Grandma Ida! Please tell me where you're sitting. I know you're here, your neighbors told me where to find you.'

My girls shake their heads in surprise. Our Ida looks around the room with all the others.

Erwin deals with this interloper, his toupee escaping, and his forehead sweating as he grabs her by the scruff of her neck. 'Out! Out of here!'

He is shoving her back toward the door.

She yells. 'Ida Franz! Stand up, darn it!'

The whole room turns toward table number three; us. We are a known entity. We immediately swivel to our Ida as well.

Ida looks puzzled. 'What . . .? I have no idea who that troublemaker is.' But she stands up anyway. 'I'm Ida Franz. Who wants to know?'

With that, the girl pulls away from flustered Erwin, who has loosened his grip at this revelation, and briskly heads toward us.

We have become the Entertainment Segment for the lunch crowd. The entire room zooms in and fastens its orbs on our little table. We are the center of attention. Cold cuts will turn warm. Hot plates will cool down. Gossip rules.

Ida, still standing, puts her hands on her hips. 'So, speak up – who are you?'

The young girl looks Ida up and down, as if she were measuring the hostile woman for a hanging. 'I'm Tori—'

Ida snaps, instantly turtle-jawed. 'Aha! I don't have any grandchild named *Tori*.' With that, she sits back down in a dramatic huff. And folds her arms in a close-the-discussion position. To prove her disinterest, she unfolds said arms in order to take a dainty bite of her blintz.

'Mom and Dad named me Gloria. You know why.'

Ida gawks. Something registers.

Bella whispers to Sophie, 'How can she be Gloria and Tori at the same time? Is that legal?'

Sophie shushes her. 'Just listen.'

'I changed that name, because I hated it.'

Ida's mouth drops open, a tidbit of blintz hanging from her lips. She clambers up, pulling away from her chair. She reaches out eagerly to the girl, then stops short, as if a light bulb turned off.

Ida, being Ida, the Ida I know, assumes nothing at face value. She worries about being embarrassed before an audience. Or about being taken advantage of; she will not jump immediately into any new situation. Or accept any passing child?

Tori's arms have opened up for her as well, then she stops, startled, that her grandmother is no longer moving toward her. The face that faces her is closed.

7

'Okay, Tori, or whoever you are – I'll admit to having a grandchild named Gloria, but how do I know it's the real you?'

My girls are surprised. Even I am astonished at Ida's odd response. But then again, typical from Ida Franz, our Queen of Distrust.

Sophie and Bella are clutching each other. They are excited by watching a happy longtime reunion with a family member. About to happen before their very eyes, like in all the romance books they read. They are ready to shed tears of joy, but what's this? Why has Ida stopped short?

Tori's mood turns angry. It's as if she had been willing to meet her grandmother halfway, but instead, the woman is denying her.

Ida, 'Before I commit to knowing you, prove who you are; where do you come from?'

Tori stiffens, her eyes blazing. By the looks of her, I have the feeling this girl has been through a lot. I don't think she'll stand for this kind of treatment.

'What's wrong with you?' Tori responds, her voice gritty. 'You want to play games? I just traveled three thousand miles to see you.' She sneers. 'I come from California. I live on the street you lived on before you skipped town. Want me to name it? Brimfield Avenue in Panorama City. Good enough proof? Want me to describe our house – the kitchen, with the ugly boring avocado fridge and stove? The living room with that scratchy orange rag rug; how about our one and only pukey-green bathroom with the little yellow ducky perched on the tub? Should I describe the rest of that dump?' She stops, choking on her rage.

Ida pales. She's caught in her own trap and I think she doesn't know how to get out of it gracefully. Her arms drop to her side.

Weakly, 'It sounds familiar.'

I'm stunned. What is our friend doing? She's lived among us for fifteen years, a woman of mystery, not wanting to speak about her past. Her past is now here and she rejects it?

I glance around the room. The diners haven't stopped staring; eyes jumping from each of us at our table, measuring our reactions, reminding me of watching a tennis match. Surely this girl is telling the truth. Why is Ida behaving so weirdly?

Desperation now. Ida can't let go. 'How do I know you didn't change places with my granddaughter somewhere and are taking her place? I don't recognize you.'

I look at my friend, askance. Ida, what are you doing?

The girl's lips manage to form a smile. It isn't a pretty sight. There's fury in that pretense of pleasure. 'I wouldn't wonder. The last time you saw me I was two years old.'

Something strange is going on here. Why is the girl staying and listening to this? Why does Ida deny her? What does this stranger want?

'Come on, Granny, cut it out, you know it's me!'

After struggling with the last shreds of an inside-her-head battle, Ida gives up and jumps up again. She reaches out once more and hugs the girl, who hugs her back. But only for a moment, then the girl turns away. 'My grandbaby,' Ida cries, still holding on. 'My darling grandbaby. It's really you!'

9

Sophie, Bella, Evvie and I are amazed. Interesting to note about that hug. As if the child really cares, but mustn't let herself show that she cares.

Tori pulls away and, like a melting ice cube, announces, 'I would have stayed away from you forever, old lady, but I have no choice. They're coming after me to kill me. Grandma Ida, you have to help me.'

One
What's with the Weird-Looking Kid?

They're still at it when we arrive back home and tiptoe over to where the action is, so as not to break their concentration. The Every Afternoon Blackjack Game in the Garden. Otherwise known as free-for-all kibitzers and killers.

The kibitzers are those residents of Lanai Gardens who have nothing better to do than to watch the cheating players, cheer their favorites on and wait for the fights to ensue.

The killer card players consist of Hy Binder, aka, Mr Annoyance and his forever clingy wife, Lola; chubby Tessie and her relatively new husband, short Sol Spankowitz (a month, and she still won't trust him, reminding him daily of his peccadilloes as the infamous peeping Tom), and Joe Markowitz, Evvie's loving husband, former ex, now her newly re-wed. And my new husband, the infinitely patient Jack Langford, stuck in his unwanted job of dealer and banker.

Anyway, here go the card players, and their shtick. Hy and Lola don't bother to conceal the fact that they discuss each other's hand with every deal. World-class cheaters.

Sol has trouble holding his cards because 'pleasingly plump' Tessie (as she refers to her 250 lethal pounds) won't let go of Sol's playing hand, as if afraid he'll fly off to some panting senior hotsy-totsy babe in the wings waiting to pull up her bedroom shade for him to look in.

Evvie's Joe's every other impatient comment is, 'So play, already', as each decision is agonized over, while my Jack, waiting to deal, reads a book to pass the endless boring time. Jack has been awarded with this choice job since he was once a cop and can be trusted to hold the bank money. All eight dollars of it.

We have arrived in time to hear a familiar litany:

Hy, 'I told you to stand with the fourteen, sweetness.'

Lola, 'But I was sure I'd get a seven, dearest one.'

Joe (shouting), 'Twenty-four is not twenty-one. Lay your cards down already!'

Hy, 'Don't rush, my adorable one. She needs to count the cards herself.'

Joe (apoplectic, shouting), 'Fourteen and ten is twenty-four!'

Lola (still counting), 'Now you made me lose my place.' (She starts over), 'One, two three . . .'

Tessie, '*We* have a real twenty-one here, don't we, pussycat?' Tessie pinches Sol's arm, yelling, 'BINGO!' as Sol screams in pain, dropping his cards onto the grass.

Joe (to Jack), 'Do something before I kill them.'

Jack looks up from his book. 'Just as soon as I finish the chapter.'

At this point they all glance up, realizing we've arrived home.

Joe, free at last, throws down his cards, gets up and hugs Evvie. 'Good brunch, hon?'

'Unusual,' she answers as she squeezes him back.

Jack closes his book, equally relieved. He looks toward the two annoying couples, and hums under his breath, '*What I do for love.*'

I smile, 'You had your choice. These momzer misfits or the girls' deli celebration.'

'You left me Hobson's Choice, no choice at all.'

At my age, to find a smart, literate, handsome guy, who loves me as much as I love him. What are the odds?

Suddenly Hy is pointing. 'Who's that? What was that? Who's that running after Ida? She looks like some bag lady's kid.'

Sol says, 'I didn't see nothing.'

Tessie asks puzzled, 'Ida picked up somebody on the street?'

Lola never says much when Hy's around. There's only room for one ego.

I don't bother to answer their questions. Sometimes they just like hearing themselves talk.

Ida, pushing Tori, runs up the steps of our building. Building Q.

Sophie and Bella laugh. Sophie informs Hy, 'A surprise. A mystery guest! You'll love it.'

No they won't. I know better.

Two
Tori takes a Shower,
Ida Paces

We are walking back toward our apartments when Evvie glances up, then elbows me into looking up also. Ida is half hanging over our third-floor landing, arms whirling like windmills gone crazy.

'Come up. I need you!' Ida shouts.

A quick consultation. The guys want to know if they should get involved, or is this some kind of girls' thing.

'Well, sort of,' Evvie offers.

'Can it wait until after my shuffleboard game?' Joe wants to know.

'I'll fill you in later,' she says, knowing him all too well. He sees us as nosy bodies getting involved in other people's affairs. And having a Private Eye business that justifies our right to interfere. He trots off, relieved.

Jack eyes me, curious. 'What's this about? Want me to join you, or am I to be excused also?'

'I'll fill you in on the way up.'

'I guess that's a yes.'

And I do update him. It's a short ride up to the third floor, so I give him the elevator pitch. 'A teenager came up to our table at The Continental;

she called Ida her grandmother. Suspicious Ida made her prove who she was. What was most amazing and frightening is that the girl told Ida that some mysterious "they" were going to kill her.'

My husband's former detective antenna immediately perks up and – no surprise – he is intrigued. And we arrive at Ida's apartment. Which is next door to ours.

Ida whisks us in, whispering, 'I insisted she take a shower. I had to shove her into the tub. She positively smells!' Ida wrings her hands. 'I don't need this. I absolutely don't. This is not the way I'd imagined my granddaughter.'

'Hey, Granny Goose, where did you hide my gear?' Tori shouts from the other room.

Ida continues to whisper, 'I tossed the clothes she was wearing into the burn barrel. They were disgusting. I hate to think of what's in her backpack.'

'I heard that . . .' Tori enters, dripping water on the living-room floor, naked as naked can be. '. . . So, what am I supposed to wear?'

A group gasp.

To be polite, Jack turns his back.

Evvie rolls her eyes.

I shake my head. Oh, my, what is going on here?

Ida shrieks, and runs over to the girl, throwing herself at her, trying to cover whatever exposed body parts she can.

Tori clutches Ida. 'C'mon, give your grandbaby a nice hug.' She tries to hold onto Ida, but Ida pushes her naked body away.

15

She yelps, 'Back! Back in my bedroom! In my closet. A robe!'

For a moment, it looks as if Tori meant it, but it looked more like a piece of drama. Am I right, Tori?

Ida may be pushing, but the girl is back-pedaling, taking in the newcomers with interest.

Evvie laughs. She's the kind of woman who finds humor anywhere.

Tori winks at Jack. With a smirk she calls out to him, 'Whoever you are, if you were only sixty years younger . . .'

Proud of her clever exit line, she bolts out of the room, leaving Ida groaning and Jack hiding a smile.

'Well?' I say nonchalantly to my husband.

'Well,' Jack says, equally unflappable. No ruffle from him. He's seen just about everything as a New York cop, and nothing surprises him. Except me and the wonder of our finding love so late in life. That did raise an eyebrow at the time.

Ida kneels on the floor, hair wildly flopping out of her bun and over her face, as she mops up the moisture with paper towels. 'What am I supposed to do with her? You should have heard her just a moment ago. A mouth like a toilet. I told her – one more nasty word out of her and I was going to wash her mouth out with soap.'

'I asked her what brand,' Tori says as she hops back into the living room wearing Ida's old green chenille robe. I think Ida's had that robe for fifty years; the woman throws nothing away.

Skinny girl, this young stranger; she swims inside it.

Tori continues. 'My other grandmother used Fels Naptha. Or was it some plain old dishwasher soap? Not that it ever shut me up.' She fairly spits. 'Just make sure you keep out of my backpack!'

Tori leaps up onto the couch, sitting Indian-style, as once again Ida stares in dismay. 'Sit straight, with your legs down on the floor.'

Tori, enjoying her grandmother's angst, ignores her and turns to me. 'So cray Gladdy-o, who's the hot old dude?'

I look at Evvie as if to ask if she understands what the girl is saying. Evvie shakes her head and jots something down in her little notebook, the one she carries with her everywhere. A holdover from her days when she wrote our local in-house newsletter.

'Yo? Speak up.' Tori tilts her head at me, like some curious little bird interested at who's climbed into her nest. I guess that means she's still waiting for me to identify Jack.

'This is my husband, Jack. I thought since you mentioned something about killing, a former policeman might come in handy.'

Tori claps her hands. 'I love it! I'm here two seconds and you call the fuzz.'

I add, 'You said you were in danger.'

'If I wanted a cop, I would have picked a young one. That's for damn sure.' Tori looks him up and down. 'Ya really are a cop?'

Jack shrugs. 'I'm afraid so.'

Tori is surprised. She didn't expect this. She

17

hesitates. I can almost hear the wheels turning. How will she use this information?'

Tori meets Jack's shrug with one of her own. 'Oh, well, ya wun a da 5.0. So, let the interrogation begin.'

I can't resist asking, 'Why are you so angry at your grandmother?'

Tori, poses, hands on hips. 'I could tell you why. Maybe I should tell you why, but then again, I won't. She knows very well why I'm angry. And for good reason.' She turns to Ida. 'Granny, tell them why I might possibly hate you. Tell them!'

We all turn to Ida, who cowers.

Ida speaks so low, we can barely hear her. 'Can't I tell you how sorry I am?'

She snorts, 'Too late Granny, too late.'

Three
Tori Spins a Tale

We sit in our Florida room, as the sun room is often called. Jack and I are usually here at this hour for a quiet after-dinner time, sipping our favorite Pinot Grigio wine and watching another glorious sunset. However, this afternoon we watched Ida have a hissy fit watching Tori bounce up and down on her precious velveteen sofa. Too nervous for any more conversation, it was agreed we'd rest awhile, meet again after dinner and have that discussion then.

18

The 'rest' period didn't seem to help. Ida still looks like a wreck. I can't recall ever seeing her like this. She must have mixed feelings. Here is the beloved grandchild whom she never expected to see again, but this girl is nothing like she could have imagined.

Not that they were invited, but seeing Ida, Evvie and Tori enter our apartment, Sophie and Bella scurry to join us and the sun room is now crowded. There is a chattering of voices and a clattering of chairs as the group decides on where they will sit. With bumping into one another as they arrange and rearrange my wicker furniture, with many an *oops* and *so sorrys*, finally they get seated.

Sophie and Bella had made a quick trip back to their own apartments and brought over a bag of after-dinner popcorn and are treating this as a party. They dump their goodies on my coffee table and Tori immediately grabs a handful. Which makes me wonder how dinner went. Did Tori refuse Ida's food in an act of passive-aggressive behavior, and is now hungry? I wouldn't put it past her. This is an angry girl.

Tori is still wearing Ida's bathrobe and I shudder to think she still has no clothes on underneath it. I'm sure Sophie, our clothing maven, will pick up on this. And she does.

'Is that Ida's chenille? Why are you wearing her robe?' Sophie asks.

'Yeah, why?' adds her Bobbsey Twin, Bella.

'Because bad Granny threw most of my clothes away.'

19

'Why did she do that?' the twosome ask in cadence.

'Never mind,' grumps Ida. 'Let's get this over with.'

Tori plops down onto my hand-woven Indian-style rug, looking up at Jack. 'Watcha lookin' at, pops?' says she who is doing the staring. Then another quick glance up at me, hoping to get a response this time. Not a chance.

Jack is sitting in his favorite armchair and all eyes focus on him. 'Okay, Tori, talk to us.' His voice is soft and mild.

Tori preens importantly, changing her tone to sincere. 'Oooh, look at you. The only Arab and his harem. It's not much of a story. I thought it was about time I visited my dear grandmother in Florida. I hadn't seen her in sooo long.'

The sudden proverbial melting of butter in the mouth has us astounded. Evvie's look wants to know what's with the sudden sweet-talk?

Ida is flummoxed. Suddenly her grandchild is polite?

I wonder what Tori is up to. I remind her of the killers she mentioned this morning who were coming after her. 'I thought you were frightened.'

I get a toothy, cheesy smile in return. 'Perhaps a bit of an overreaction. Just a little story to entertain. Clever, huh?'

Evvie and I exchange glances. All of a sudden she sounds like a child prodigy. Or maybe an actress. What happened to the teen-speak?

Jack asks her, 'What does that mean, an "overreaction"?'

She stretches cat-like after drinking cream.

20

'Wellll,' she drags it out. 'I was hitch-hopping rides across the country. Having the best time in a little town of La Mesa in New Mexico. Met some really cute guys in a band, four brothers, especially one of them named Luke.' Tori blushes, quickly going past that. 'And most of the people were sooo kind, but every so often one might make a bad judgment call. There were these three other guys in this mysterious-looking car wanted to pick me up. I admit I was a little impressed, a big SUV with sexy dark windows . . . but then I found out that they had these tacky tats. Can you believe – Hickory and Dickory and Doc, one on each guy's arm?' A little batting of the eyelashes. 'Dix would have been enough.'

Sophie and Ida are shocked by what they think she means.

'You know how men can get!' This line is sent out to Jack, suggesting shared sophistication. She moves her robe enough to show a bit of bare leg.

'I may have sent out the wrong signals. A little too much *vino*. Maybe a dash of hash.' She giggles. 'And when I refused their naughty advances . . .'

Jack says drily, 'That's when they threatened to kill you.'

'Something like that.'

Jack gets up out of his chair. 'Well, you're safe here. I suppose my expertise is not needed. Time to watch a little TV.'

The party ends abruptly. Tori hesitates, realizes her fifteen minutes of attention is over, and races to the front door. Ida hurries after her. Sophie and Bella are right behind them. Bella calls out,

'Thanks for a lovely evening. You can keep the rest of the popcorn.'

For a moment after we hear the door slam, no one speaks. Jack is back in his chair. 'Too bad I no longer drink hard liquor or smoke . . . Right now, I crave both.'

Evvie shakes her head. 'I expected her to say, "I'm ready for my close-up, Mr DeMille." What a performance!'

'What on earth could that be about? Cruella turns into Snow White?'

'Well, I could use a drink.' Evvie reaches into the mini-fridge and makes herself a gin and tonic. 'Wow, Ida never saying a word. That's not the Ida we know.'

I muse, 'We didn't imagine it. That child was terrified in the deli. Why the sudden turnaround?'

Jack jokes, 'Perhaps she wanted to spare my tender feelings.' Serious now, 'She's not ready to talk.'

Evvie digs into her purse and takes out her notepad. 'I went online to look up all those funny things she said earlier. I googled Teen Expressions and got some answers. Gladdy, when she called you *cray*. That means crazy.'

'How nice for me.'

'*Hot* means hot stuff.'

'That's gotta be me,' says Jack with a smirk. 'What was that *ya da* stuff?'

She reads. '*Ya wun a da 5.0*? You'll love this. *You're one of the 5.0* refers to the old TV series *Hawaii 5.0*. Meaning, so you're a cop.'

I comment, 'This child is a female Dr Jekyll and Mr Hyde. One thing we already know about

22

her, she is precocious and very intelligent for her age. Probably high IQ.'

Evvie adds, 'Smart enough to toy with us and test us.'

Jack wonders, 'I believe she didn't lie about someone trying to kill her, so why now the play-acting? She knows I'm a cop. I could help her.'

I guess, 'Perhaps to cover a lot of pain? Perhaps first she needs to trust us. When Ida moved here fifteen or so years ago, she confided in me, something she didn't want anyone else to know. She originally came from California, where she lived quite close to her children and grandchildren. Her husband, Murray, had died a year before. There were other sad happenings in her family. Something had gone very wrong, but she wouldn't tell me any more.'

Evvie, 'It must have been something serious to cause so much rage in that child.'

I add, 'Serious enough for Ida to run away, leaving behind the grandchildren she loved. But why? Ida has hidden her past all these years. Telling us she just wanted to forget. Now, Tori is here. Maybe she'll tell us the rest.'

'Poor Ida,' I continue. 'That kid has a love-hate relationship with her grandmother. So why does she come to live with her? And what about the danger she fears? Is it real? How do we get Tori to share this with us?'

Jack tosses us some biting wit. 'By interrogating her without me in the room? I'm just too much "eye candy" for her to handle? I don't want to torture the little flirt. Let me know when she's ready.' With that, he laughs on his way out of the room.

I throw a handful of the popcorn after him, causing him to duck and run.

Four
Who Peed in the Pool?

I see Sophie pounding on my kitchen window, so that must be Bella ringing the doorbell. I quickly throw my cover-up shirt over my swimsuit and hop into my flip-flops. I can hear Jack calling from the bedroom, 'I knew it. They're three minutes early.'

'Don't worry, I'll go outside and wait there for you. They're just excited.'

'I'm not coming out until I've had my coffee.'

It's a typical sizzler of a day, with the temperature in the 90s and the humidity at 85 per cent – that's why swimming and swimming events are held early in the morning.

Sure enough, the 'twins' are eagerly waiting right outside our door. As usual, the two of them are doing their peas-in-a pod routine. Sea-green swim outfits, and sea-green flip-flops are the color-coordination of the day.

Lately, Sophie has been suffering with weak legs; she is using a cane more and more, and even the cane has green ribbons.

And here come Evvie and Ida, with Tori lagging behind.

My neighbors are already poised downstairs or on their walkways and landings, or peeking out windows waiting to watch the big event.

Once a year we have the Skip to My Lou race, which awards a prize for the first person to skip his or her way from Buildings P and Q and jump into the pool. For a group our age, it's a relatively short race. What we lack in mileage, we make up in laughing. Years ago, somebody named Lou had started it and the name stuck. So did the game. And that old song. And, as in every year, those who need canes and walkers are eligible to a three-foot head start. All our cars have been moved from the front of our buildings to provide skipping space.

'Who you betting on this year, Glad?' Sophie wants to know.

'Naturally, Hy, he's won the last seven years in a row. The even money is on him.'

'I'm going with Lola to place.'

'Also a sure thing.'

Bella tee-hees. 'Yeah, she holds onto the back of his trunks, so he can pull her in with him when he jumps.'

Evvie adds, 'Even my Joe skips, though he usually comes in last. Though he tries real hard.'

We clutch our betting tickets. Toby, a ninety-three-year-old newcomer with artistic abilities, designed our programs to resemble the ones at Hialeah, our famous local racetrack. With write-ups of the players, and their odds. Jeffrey, our favorite Canadian snowbird, an accountant from Toronto, is in charge of all the betting money. All bets are one buck each. Money goes to charity.

25

Our whistle blower, Ernie, from Building T, stands at attention, to the left of the excited, waiting skippers.

Jack comes out on our landing with his coffee cup. Tori immediately sidles up to him. 'How come you aren't racing?' she asks to get his attention.

Putting her on, 'I'm more of the intellectual type.'

Tori, eager now, 'Really? Me, too.'

I tune in, amused. Jack is going to trap her.

Jack pretends enthusiasm. 'I've just finished James Joyce's *Ulysses* for the fourth time. Still can't put it down. Of course, you've read it?'

She looks chagrined. 'I've been too busy lately to read.'

'Oh, so sorry. Though the Irish dialect makes for tough reading, don't you think?'

I give Jack a look that says – you should be ashamed of yourself; she's only a child.

Tori smiles shyly, wanting to please him. 'But it is on my to-read list. That's the one with his character, Leopold Bloom, and his life in one day in Dublin. I have the paperback and I'm really looking forward to it.'

Jack turns red. Tori is absolutely right. He changes the subject quickly. 'So, what have you been doing since you got here? Sightseeing?'

Tori tunes him out. 'Yes, a little bit of this and a little bit of that.'

By now all spectators are lined up. Everyone is in bathing suits, prepared for the Giving of the Awards swim party afterwards.

Tori, asks, with pretended interest, 'What's with the yelling and cheering? Why is everyone

26

outside and who are those weirdoes lined up down there?'

Evvie explains Skip to My Lou to her.

She laughs out loud. 'This is a race with all those oldies with canes and walkers? They're going to skip? *Skip!* That's your idea of racing? That's the stupidest thing I've ever heard.'

'We enjoy it, wait till you're our age,' Ida says with that same flat tone, so unusual for her. Tori must still be giving her a hard time. I look to Ida as if asking – has she learned anything new about her granddaughter? Why she's here? Ida shakes her head. Nothing.

'Two minutes,' Ernie announces.

Evvie is pointing. 'Look what our resident egomaniac is wearing.'

She doesn't have to identify Hy. We all know who it is. Our bantam-sized neighbor is showing off as usual. Over his hairy chest, he wears all seven of his fake gold medals on their equally fake gold chains. He is bowing and waving his Miami Dolphins cap to his fans. Stepford Wifey, Lola, gazes adoringly at her champion.

Joe, waiting, does knee bends. Evvie waves her home-made flag at her hubby. He waves back.

Tori watches everyone as if she were at the zoo, and these were the inhabitants. She mimics ape noises and scratches her underarms. Then switches to laughing hyena sounds. The new kid on the block is actually letting herself have a good time. For a moment, I can see the eager child in her.

Then she munches on what she identifies as her power bar.

27

Ida whispers low to me, 'She doesn't like my cooking.'

Evvie and I exchange meaningful glances. Ida is considered our best cook. Unkind and aggressive behavior is going on in that apartment. She is punishing her grandmother. Why?

We lean in on our railings, ready for the race to start. Tori squeezes herself next to Jack. Jack looks at me over her head, amused by her obviousness.

'Ready,' Ernie calls out and lifts his whistle, and the team straightens up. As best they can with creaking bones. 'Get set,' he shouts even louder. The able skippers, caners and walkers lean inward, ready, willing, though I'm not sure able.

The whistle is blown, loud and shrill; the skippers take off. Everyone on the sidelines bursts into song:

'Skip, skip, skip to my Lou (repeat three times)

'Flies in the buttermilk (repeat three times)

'Skip, skip, skip to my Lou . . .' (eight verses)

Ernie now uses his mic and gives us a skip-by-skip rundown. He imitates the colorful raspy guy he hears every week at Hialeah. 'Hy taking the lead. Lola right behind him. Joe has gotten a cramp in the leg and is falling behind. Irving is running out of breath. Helena from Building M has dropped her cane. She bends down to reach it and Mary from Building S falls over her. They both limp to a bench . . . Too bad, girls.'

Evvie sighs, tells us watchers, 'I told Joe he would be too stiff to skip! It'll be an hour in the hot tub tonight.'

28

The downstairs viewers follow the sweating skippers from the starting line, walking quickly alongside them, calling out to their favorites, singing loudly, as well. Chorus after chorus of 'Skip to My Lou'. Everyone is having a grand old time.

I am aware of the expression on Tori's face, pretending to hide her smile. She's getting a kick out of this.

Hy, ahead of the crowd as usual, hits the edge of the pool first, looks down. He hesitates for a second, sees something, tries to stop himself, waving his arms wildly, then loses his balance and falls in. Lola, holding onto his trunks, falls in right behind him. With the other ten in hot pursuit. Those with canes and walkers push their equipment aside, and jump in right behind Lola and Hy. To their instant regret.

'They're screaming,' Tori says as we hurry downstairs and are getting close to the pool fence. Like all the others, we rush along the path to the pool to keep up with the race.

Evvie comments, smiling, 'Yes, aren't they? Screaming in pleasure.'

'No, I'd say that they're screaming in terror.' Tori smiles, wickedly.

And suddenly there is a mad scrambling and splashing as the ones in the pool try to crawl back out, colliding with those still jumping in. Smacking and elbowing when someone gets in their way. Hy, loudest, pushing hardest. Pandemonium. Shouts are heard inside and outside the pool.

'Alligator!'

'Help! Alligator in the pool!'
'Get away from me!'
'Get out!'
'Somebody call 911.'
'Somebody call a wrangler!'
'Alligator! Ugh!'
'*Oy vey!*'
'Stop hurting me!'
'You're stepping on my wooden leg!'
'Get out – don't get in!'
'Ohmigod!'

The rest of us arrive at the pool, trying to see what's happening. Horrified at the panic. Hands waving helplessly at the carnage about to occur.

Hy, always with the right words for the occasion, screams at them. 'Don't just stand there, *shmucks!* Do something!' He crawls backward to the steps, shoving others aside, like a football wide receiver running for the touchdown.

'Wait, listen!' It's Charles from building U standing close on the grassy edge of the pool. 'It's dead! You have a dead alligator at the bottom of the pool.'

Everything stops. All looking down from whatever their perch.

Smiling.

Nervous laughter.

Hysterical sobbing.

'Thank God!'

'Disgusting, I'll never swim in here again.'

'We're okay, it's dead. We're alive!'

'It must be a female to be so ugly.' That, naturally, from Hy.

Those still in the pool swim or walk around this huge 'scaly thing', examining it with scholarly interest. The terrorized have become the Nature Channel.

'Where did it come from?'

'How did it get in?'

'It wasn't here last night.'

'How long has it been there?'

'Ugly,' again Hy.

'Must be an 800-pounder.'

'Thirty feet long, I bet.'

Hy, taking charge again, now safe on the grassy edge, calls out, 'Somebody phone for a handler to get this disgusting lizard out of here?'

Lola cries, 'Hy, honey-bun. I'm stuck! Pull me out.' But he's too busy giving orders.

Suddenly, Phil, from Building H, who had been helping lift Sonya from Building J, up onto the pool rim, drops the terrified woman back into the water. He shrieks, 'Omigod, it isn't dead!' Phil desperately tries to scrabble up the pool wall, clawing uselessly, and praying at the same time.

The alligator's eyes slowly open.

'It must have been sleeping!'

'It's waking up!'

'Get out! Get out!'

'Oh, save me!'

'Out! Out! Out!'

'*Oy vey!*'

Nature Channel now becomes the Sluggish Flight of the Zombies as they splash crazily in their attempts to re-scramble their way out.

The panicked watchers on deck, trying to help, throw things at the alligator. Webbed beach

31

chairs, chaise lounges, puffy pillows, mini-tables, snorkels, sneakers, anything and everything; trying to distract the monster. Mostly hitting the skippers. Brave do-gooders, mostly the Canadians, reach into the dangerous waters, pulling helpless women out.

Everyone on deck is running in different directions. This goes on for a dreadful half-hour. Finally all the terrified skippers are out of the pool.

Hooray, the professional wranglers have arrived, amazingly fast, and take charge. They tell us that our alligator looks like he's been pickled by the chlorine, which slowed him down. Lucky for all.

Everyone watches, gasping, as the alligator, now caught, with jaws tied shut, slimily climbs up the steps, out of the pool, and is carted away in the wranglers' truck.

There is much relieved laughter, and then Tori shouts, 'Cool!' So, the California girl allows herself to have fun, after all. Is there, somewhere inside that seemingly troubled child, a happy little girl trying to come out?

The Awards pool party afterwards is an almost no-show. Thank God no one died, drowned or was bitten. Or eaten. Lots of people are hurting from bruises brought on by their hapless flailing, fellow skippers.

Most everyone has gone home to either rest and/or take tranquilizers. Or call their lawyers. Except for our group with Hy, who demands his eighth fake gold medal.

Hy suddenly notices Tori, especially when she takes off Ida's swim top and reveals the smallest bikini in the world.

'Hot diggity,' Hy says, everyone guessing his meaning.

A few still enthralled people call out to us sarcastically, as they exit our perimeter. 'See you later, alligator.' Hy, of course has to add, 'In a while, crocodile.' But Tori gets in the last word again. 'Dorks.'

Part Two
The Past Reviled

Five

Tori's Story – The Church
of the Blessed Child

Six months before

Tori, with one hand, tried to raise the small-hinged, stuck window a little higher. She needed more air. Never easy, since the church located in Van Nuys, in a downtrodden neighborhood, is so old and made of such ratty wood; she'd only get splinters again. It always gave her the creeps being in this awful, stinking bathroom. She gave up on the window and kicked at the toilet plunger at her feet, trying to punt it far away from her. Smelly and full of crap. This place made her constantly scratch her body, sure there were creepy crawlers on her.

Her cheap cell phone, with its old-fashioned flip-flop cover, is slowly dying out on her. Oh, how she envied all the kids at school with their iPhones. But her stingy grandparents, they never spent a nickel on her unless absolutely necessary.

Tori felt her sister getting impatient and wanting to hang up. 'Marilyn, I'm begging you. I can't live with them another minute.'

'We've been over it a hundred times. I just don't have the room and Tom . . .'

'Yeah, I know Tom can't stand me.'

'Well, you don't make it easy.'

'You got out. You had to marry a dumb-dumb so you could escape, but at least you're free.'

'Yeah, free. I'm paying for it now.'

'I'll sleep on the couch.'

'You can't. Billy wets the bed every night and ends up on it.'

'A sleeping bag in the garage. I'll sleep on the lawn. Anything,' unable to hide the desperation in her voice. 'When I move in, I'll be so polite to Tom, he won't even know I'm there. And I won't use bad language in front of the kids.'

'Please, stop! You know I can't. And don't keep calling Shirley. You know what a mess she made of her life.'

'Gloria! Aren't you finished cleaning yet?' Her grandmother shouted from the inside of the church proper. 'You better not be on that phone!'

'Aren't you finished cleaning yet,' she mimicked, imitating the elderly woman's nasal, rasping voice. She whispered, 'It's Tori, why won't she remember, Tori! I hate that damn Gloria. What kind of family makes a child scrub bathrooms every Sunday, especially disgusting ones like this one? Why, it's Maxel and Gertrude Steiner, poster grandparents from hell!'

Marilyn's voice softened. 'I know how bad it is. I remember it well.'

'No, you don't get it. You refuse to believe me how much worse things are; the old crappers have turned sick and decrepit. They can hardly move and they make me do every sickening thing they want. You never had to change old people's diapers! Gross! And giving them showers, ugh. You remember the non-stop drinking and non-stop smoking? Well, it's triple bad now. I'll probably die of lung cancer before I'm twenty. And the shouting. Neither one can hear worth a damn anymore, so it's screaming at each other. The neighbors have called the police.'

Marilyn interrupted. 'You'll escape soon. But promise me, not like I did. You're smart; you can get a scholarship in just about any school with your grades.'

'But that's still two years away. One more day and I might murder them.' She recited, sing-song, 'Lizzie Borden took an ax, gave her mother forty whacks, when she'd seen what she had done, gave her father forty-one.' She was crying now. 'At least we three girls used to have each other.'

'Dear, I'm so sorry, but I'm hanging up, now. Say your prayers and God will help you.'

'I need a miracle,' she said to the dead phone.

Tori heard the next loud shout, knowing that it would be her grandfather this time. They took turns. 'The parishioners will be here soon,' Maxel shouted, way too loud. 'Clean yourself up and get out.'

She didn't bother to answer but headed for the filthy sink. As the tears rolled down her face, she cried out, as if anyone could hear, 'You were the one who loved us. Who made us laugh. Who sang us to sleep with sweet lullabies. You left your grandchildren to these monsters. Grandma Ida, why did you abandon us?'

Six

Tori's Story – Panorama City

Five months before

The street darkened as she walked from the bus stop to their house at the end of Brimfield Avenue. She kept her eyes always alert in this crummy neighborhood. There were dimly lit, small, box houses, surrounded by six-foot-tall chain-link fences with razor blades lining their tops, the smell of pot in the air, shadowy figures leaning into beat-up cars. Ominous sounds. Too loud, abrasive rap music. She walked along the edge of the gutters in case she needed to run for her life. She feared walking too close to doorways, imagining being pulled in to one of them by someone evil. She sometimes smiled at her vivid imagination. Even though afraid of the dark, and its possible dangers, she made it a habit to come home as late as she could, so as to spend as little time in that house as possible.

As she moved along, like whistling in the dark, she liked to savor the stories her sisters told her about how things were before she was born. When her family moved into what was then this sweet little tract area in Panorama City

– now a slum. Her sisters, eleven and eight years older than she, were eager to rub it in. Over and over they gleefully told her what she missed and what they had before she was born. They did it to be unkind; instead, Tori reveled in those pictures they painted. She could visualize and dream about their wonderful childhood; a real neighborhood. Families with starter homes, lawns being taken care of, charming little gardens. Lots of pets. Picnics and barbecues in back yards. Neighbors became friends, their kids walking to and from schools together. Playing in each other's yards every afternoon. With their loving grandparents living nearby.

The best part was the holidays, Mama's branch of the family – the Franz side of the family – was Jewish, and Dad's side – the Steiners – were church-goers. That meant eight nights of presents when the Hanukkah candles were lit at the Franzes', and then, the most fun of all, Christmas day at the Steiners', with mountains of presents under an over-decorated and toy-filled tree. All gone now.

What she had, instead, was always being alone. No one to play with. No one to talk to. No storybook parents or grandparents. Her childhood was something out of a Charles Dickens nightmare. That was and is her life.

Because by the time Tori was born, on that horrible day, in that awful place, an obviously unwanted child, everything went really sour. When their parents became criminals, and no longer lived at home. And Grandma Ida would soon run away.

That's when the Steiners sold their small house,

41

too, and moved in to this larger one, replacing Mom and Dad, and then Ida, to take care of the three children. They had no choice, but their resentment ran high.

Tori opened the triple-locked doors. It always reminded her that she had been told, in 'the happy time', everyone left their house and car doors unlocked. Even with the keys still on the front seats.

First she sniffed, hoping to smell something cooking. No, the usual odor of cigarette smoke and of cheap liquor. She dumped her torn school backpack near the front door and reluctantly headed for the kitchen.

Grandma Gertrude sat, as typical, in her dull brown faded wooden chair at the dull brown scarred kitchen table, its earlier shine long gone. A cigarette in one hand, the booze glass in the other. Staring into space. Nothing new about that. But this was odd – she was still wearing her morning ratty bathrobe and her feet were bare, her hair uncombed. And wait, where was Grandpa Maxel? With his stinking cigars and shouted curses?

Not that Tori cared. She peered into the beat-up fridge and dug out a rancid-smelling slice of American cheese. She scraped off the mold and slid down in her chair and chewed at it. 'Mmm, so much better than yesterday's cat food.'

No comment. None expected.

'So, Tori, beloved grandchild, how was your day at school?' Tori, a natural mimic, faked her grandmother's harsh voice perfectly.

42

Now Tori 'answering' the faux grandparent, 'It was a wonderful day. I aced my math test. Was voted the cutest girl in the entire school. The football hero asked me out on a date.'

Nothing. No response.

'So, about dinner. Where's my sirloin steak? Make sure it's medium rare this time. The last one burned. And about the baked potato with sour cream and chives. You might try cooking the potato first.'

This was the game she played with herself, having improbable conversations with those semi-conscious robots she was forced to live with.

Then she became aware of a different stench. Oh, God, urine. Her grandmother had peed herself. And that sound? Like whining. Gertrude, rocking her body and making that god-awful noise.

Tori leaped up. 'I am not going to change your bloomers, you hear! Let dear Maxel do it.'

'IN THERE!' Grandma shouted, pointing.

'IN WHERE?' Tori shouted back.

The old lady dropped the cigarette in the booze glass, dragged herself out of her chair and hobbled out of the kitchen.

'What's where?' Tori followed her through the unlit hallways. What was the old bag up to now?

They reached the bedroom, the room her parents had once slept in. Taken over years ago, after Ida left, by the Steiners.

Grandmother pointed at the bed. Where Maxel was lying, his face to the wall.

'THERE!' She screamed.

Tori leaned over the bed and shouted at her

43

grandfather. 'No, no, none of that! You're in charge of diaper-changing tonight.'

Tori pulled at him, turning the body around. His body flopping. 'I don't care how drunk you are. Get out of this bed!'

A body that showed no response no matter how hard she shook it. She finally realized that Grandpa Maxel was dead.

And behind her Grandmother Gertrude, still pointing, making that sound like a squealing pig.

Seven

Tori's Story – Grandma and Grandpa Same Night

They were back in the kitchen.

'Grandma, I'm so sorry.' Tori tried to put her arm around the shaking woman.

Her grandmother shrugged her away, and sat back down on her chair, eyes fixed on the greasy, unwashed floor. Tori went to the stove.

'Would you like some tea? Do you want me to call anyone?'

'What for? It won't help him.'

'But maybe it would be good to have someone around.' Tori was at a loss. She didn't know what to do. Or say. Hey, she thought, I'm just a kid here. I've never seen a dead person before.

'No, leave me alone.'

'You're shaking. I'll get you a blanket.'

'No, go away.'

Tori poured herself a cup of tea and placed it on the table. She lifted the half-empty bottle of whiskey and held it up toward Grandma. She brought her a barely clean glass and removed the one with the cigarette butt.

The old woman grabbed the bottle from her and poured her own drink with trembling hands. She gulped it down and tossed another. Poured yet one more.

'When did it happen? Did he just not wake up this morning?' Attempting to make small talk, knowing she was doing it wrong.

'Shut up.'

'I'm trying to help.'

'Don't bother.' She downed the third shot, and pulled herself up again.

'Where are you going?'

'To bed.'

'That's a good idea. You should get some rest.' Then, the horrible thought. 'You want me to make up a bed for you in Marilyn's old room?'

'I'm sleeping with him.'

Disturbing visions of things she'd read in books. Maybe lying in his own mess. Gross. 'I'd be glad to do it. With clean sheets.'

Grandma Gertrude shook a fist at her. 'I slept next to that man for sixty-five years. I'll die next to him.'

She started out of the room.

Tori followed after her, grabbing at her arm. 'Don't talk silly. You have a lot of years left. I'll get up real early and buy some food and I'll make you a nice breakfast.' She was summoning up every cliché she'd ever heard or read or seen in movies.

'Don't bother.'

She looked at her grandma, standing like a stone statue; glaring at her. Whispering now. 'Grandma, why do you hate me?' Somehow she finally needed to ask this question. A question hanging over her all her life.

Gertrude actually smiled, as if she had waited years for this moment. Spittle formed on her lips. 'Because it all went bad when you were born. You put a curse on us. You doomed us to this hideous life.'

Tori clutched at her stomach, as if her grandmother had stuck a knife in her gut.

As if that wasn't enough, her grandmother had more to say. 'Don't bother coming to wake me. I'm leaving with him tonight. I pray Saint Peter will be at the gates, waiting to let us into heaven.'

She watched, holding down her nausea, as Grandma Gertrude pulled off her bathrobe and climbed into the bed beside the dead man.

Tori was determined not to sleep that night. Every hour on the hour she stood at their open door and glanced down at her grandmother, her arms clutched around her dead husband's body. Tori leaned in to make sure she was breathing.

Tori finally fell asleep, in spite of not wanting to, sitting up in an armchair in her bedroom. It was nine a.m. when she finally awakened, leapt up and rushed to their bedroom.

The breathing had stopped. Her grandmother

was dead. She gasped, no, impossible! But sadly, true.

Tori's first thought, she must call the police. Then, thought again. Maybe she'd better not.

To her surprise, Tori wanted to cry. She held it back. 'I'm so sorry life was so crappy for you. Rest in peace, Grandma. Rest in peace, Grandpa.'

Eight
Tori's Story – The Sisters
Early Morning

'I can't believe my eyes! I can't believe it! Both of them dead!' Her sister, Marilyn, shook her head in disbelief. And you didn't call the police!'

'I called you.'

Shirley was holding a small pocket mirror in front of her grandmother's nose. The girls were lined up alongside the bed, staring down on this bizarre sight.

Tori had phoned her sisters and they had both dashed over. She found herself looking closely at them, something she hardly ever did. As they were getting older, they looked more alike. Marilyn at twenty-six, Shirley, twenty-three. Both were starting to get fat around the belly, like Mom. With Mom's Wicked Witch hooked nose, and her straight hair and dark coloring.

Tori felt lucky; maybe she took after Dad, not

that she'd ever seen a photo. He probably had her lighter, curly brown hair. As she watched her much older sisters pretend they cared, she thought of herself as Cinderella with those two wicked sisters. Mirror, mirror on the wall, who's the fairest one of all? She giggled. Wrong fairy tale.

Suddenly Marilyn pushed at Shirley's hand holding the mirror. 'Stop it, already.' And Tori came out of her reverie.

Shirley was miffed. 'I just wanted to make sure. I never heard of anyone saying they're going to die and then lie down and just do it!'

Marilyn turned to Tori, suspicious now. 'What did you do? You said you wanted them dead. Did you find some way to poison Grandma, so she would die, too?'

Tori thought about smacking her, then decided not to. 'Don't be an idiot. I told you exactly how it went down.'

'Grandma actually told you she was getting into the bed with him in order to die with him. Right then and there?'

'That was her story, Morning Glory. Just like Romeo and Juliet. Two dead people in spooning position. And hoped Saint Peter would let them into heaven. If it was up to me, the pearly gates would be locked and they'd be on their way to hell.'

Marilyn couldn't stand it. 'But they hated each other! I'll bet from the day they married. They never stopped cursing each other. Why would she want to die with him?'

Shirley added her bit. 'Used to throw plates at each other. I wish she had given me her Fiesta

48

Ware set of dishes, instead of breaking every-thing against the kitchen wall.'

'Why didn't you call a doctor?' Marilyn asked. 'Or the police?'

'Are you crazy? I thought about it. Their doctor could make them undead? The cops would think the same stupid thing you did and arrest me? Thanks a bunch.'

'Let's get out of here,' Shirley whined. 'I can't stand looking at them, and besides, the room smells.'

In the hallway Marilyn added, 'The whole place stinks.'

Tori pinched Marilyn's arm. 'You noticed that, did you? This is what I've been living with. You might have noticed if you ever came here to visit. And don't ask for anything to eat, or drink, there's nothing. We ran out of food stamps a week ago. I beg kids to share their lunches with me at school. A few do.'

Automatically, without even discussing it, they reached the kitchen and her two sisters sat down. Tori paced. Marilyn frowned. 'I'm sorry, Tori, I never believed you when you said it was this bad. Forgive me.'

'I forgive you.'

'Because we're much older than you, I didn't think we had anything in common.'

Shirley couldn't resist. She looked in the fridge, then closed it quickly. 'Disgusting.'

'Might have been nice if either of you ever invited me to lunch. I would never ask to be invited to come over for dinner, considering your loving husbands would be there. God forbid I might make a pass at one of them. Ugh!'

Shirley looked like she was about to argue, but Marilyn stopped her. They both knew she was right.

Her sisters sat quietly for a few minutes, lost in their own thoughts. Tori leaned her back against the kitchen sink, arms folded, ignoring the dirty dishes.

Shirley asked, 'What are you going to do?'

'What am *I* going to do? I'm the baby in the family; I'm looking to the two of you for help.'

'We could call the pastor of their church,' Shirley suggested.

'Too late to hear their final prayers.'

'We have to report their deaths to an undertaker or someone. There has to be a funeral, I guess.' Marilyn lifted her arm from the table and rubbed at a dirty stain on her elbow.

Tori jumped away from the sink and pounded on the table. 'Wait! I just realized! You better do nothing. Not until I make some kind of plan for myself.'

Shirley was confused. 'What do you mean? What plan?'

She was thinking out loud. 'They won't let me live here alone. I'm a minor. I can't move in with either of you. You made that clear. I can't live with Mom in prison, ha ha, funny! They'll drag me through those Child Services. My life will no longer be my own. What will they do? Get me adopted? Stick me in some stranger's home who'll get paid to keep me, and I bet it'll be with another pair of drunks. You can't tell anyone, not yet! I need time to think.'

50

Marilyn spoke sadly, 'You're going to run away? They'll catch you like they did all the rest of the times.'

Shirley's head hung down. 'I said something to Kip.'

Tori turned to her and shook her shoulders. 'What did you tell him?'

'Not too much.'

'What, exactly?'

Shirley hesitated. 'I told him only Grandpa was dead. I wasn't sure what you meant when you said they were both dead.'

Tori kept shaking her. 'You have to take that back!'

'I don't know how—'

Tori didn't let her finish. 'Are you sure he was listening? He usually tunes you out.'

It looked like Shirley was about to argue again, and then didn't bother. 'Well, he was working on his Harley.'

Tori relaxed. 'If he brings it up, tell him he heard you wrong.'

Shirley nodded her head. 'I'll just say he's kind of sick . . . a cold, that's it. Not that he'd care.'

Marilyn got up. 'I need to get home.'

'Me, too,' Shirley copy-catted, also getting up.

'Give me time to decide what to do.'

Tori walked them to the door. Shirley turned and headed back. 'Wait. Hang on a mo, I wanna take her Jiminy Cricket Christmas platter. She won't need it anymore.'

Tori glared at Marilyn. 'I have one idea already and you're going to help me. I want to go see

51

Mom. Maybe she'll give me an idea or something. Besides, I need to tell her I'm getting out of here.'

Marilyn backed off, half out the front door. 'No way. I've taken you enough times. I swore I'd never go to that damn prison again. I can't stand it. She's mad as a hatter.'

'You don't have to sit next to her, just go, so I can get in.'

'No. I don't know how she gets drugs and booze in that place. But she's in Looney Tunes land now. Last time she didn't even know who I was. So, definitely, not.'

'Don't mess with me now. I'm your sister. You have to do this one last thing and then you'll never see me again.'

Marilyn took Tori's hands in hers. 'I'm so sorry. About never being there for you. But I know her loyal lawyer visits her often. We don't have to.'

'I don't care. You will take me to Mom.' She pointed a thumb back toward the bedroom. 'They're ripening pretty fast in here.'

They turned at the sound of a crash. Shirley walked back to them, with a shrug, looking sheepish. 'Dropped it. No biggie, they'll think it goes with all the other plates Grandma trashed on the floor.'

Marilyn pushed Shirley out the door. 'Moron!'

Tori called after her as she headed for her car. 'I mean it, Marilyn. Hurry. I need to get out of here!'

She closed the door, stood there for a while, thinking. Well, first things first. Dear Gertrude and Maxel, those cheapskates, boasted how they never trusted banks. Time to search for her inheritance.

Nine
Tori's Story – Off to Jail We Go

Two weeks before

As Tori watched hysterically, Marilyn drove round and round the prison's vast parking area searching for an empty spot.

Tori was practically jumping out of her seat. 'Find something, dammit. We'll be late.' She was aware of sweating in these too-tight, uncomfortable clothes, fearful her underarm stains would show. The weather around Stockdale was hot and sticky and Marilyn's crappy air-conditioner hardly worked.

Tori pinched her arm. 'Hurry. Over there. Someone is leaving.'

Marilyn kept driving in the same direction.

Tori punched her shoulder. 'What are you doing? Can't you make a U-ey? It's only four cars down.'

'Yeah, sure, but it's an illegal turn. Want me to get arrested?' Marilyn hiccupped with laughter. 'Good one. We're already in a prison yard; they can just drop me directly into a cell. Maybe I can room with Mom.'

She swiveled, looking forward. 'Wait, never mind, look, there, three down, your side, another opening.'

Marilyn sped up and waited for the driver to back out.

Tori looked into the driver-side window of the beat-up old Volvo. 'Damn, it's some old biddy driving. She'll take forever.'

'Don't get your knickers in a twist.' Marilyn laughed again. 'Grandma Gertrude used to say that.'

'Don't even mention her. Don't tell Mom she's dead. Don't tell Mom anything. Pretend everything is okay.'

'All right, already. I have no intention of saying a word. I'm warning you again, she won't know who we are.'

Tori held her breath as the elderly woman maneuvered agonizingly slowly. 'She's so damn slow.'

'Try to stay calm.'

Tori recited as if it were a mantra. 'Five more minutes. Five more minutes and they won't hold our VPASS! Four more minutes! They'll toss us into the "walk-up" line and we'll be here for hours. You know how strict they are about being here at least thirty minutes before an appointment! Three more minutes!'

The old lady finally managed to leave the parking space. Marilyn maneuvered her way in.

Tori mumbled. 'When I think of how much work it was to get this pass, just so we wouldn't have to wait in line!'

'Fix your hair. We've arrived.'

Tori fairly leapt out of the car, pointing. 'Let's haul ass, dammit. What are you doing?' She couldn't believe what she was seeing as Marilyn took the time to lock her car door.

Tori shrieked. 'Someone's gonna steal it here?'

Tori drummed her finger on the plain pine table in the visiting room. Marilyn sat several seats away from her. 'What's taking so long?'

Marilyn commented. 'It's a good thing you're only fifteen and not sixty. You might have had a heart attack by now. Try to relax.'

'Why don't you sit closer?'

'I told you, I'm pretending I'm not here.'

Tori glanced around the other tables, where visitors spoke quietly with their convict relatives. The huge room smelled heavily of air freshener, the cheap kind they used in old toilets. There were no windows. Just dreary beige walls and beige tables and beige chairs.

Every time the door opened, Tori looked up expecting Mom, only to be disappointed. She glanced away again as this latest female was brought in. Wishing she hadn't had to leave her brand-new iPhone at the door. She giggled. Of course Marilyn wanted to know how she could afford a new phone. Tori told her exactly where the money came from that paid for the phone and all the other new goodies, like that brand-new computer and fancy new backpack.

Marilyn hissed at her. 'Psst, there she is.'

Tori looked again at the same woman weaving her way in. She was horrified; it was as if she

55

no longer recognized her mother. Skeleton-thin, patches of gray hair in among the baldness. Bent over, looking down at the floor, fists clenched. Clothes that barely hung on her emaciated body. She looked ages older than her fifty-two.

Tori caught the eye of Dix, the prison guard she usually saw on these visits. Big and bulky like many of them were. Mean-looking. But he was always nice to her. Giving her the latest info on how her mother was doing. Mom had never been as bad as this. She felt instant guilt. Lately her visits had become less and less important to her. The guard nodded, understanding her shock; he knew how sad it was.

Moving at her very slow pace, Dix gently brought Helen Steiner to the table and helped seat her directly across from Tori. The woman kept her fists clenched and in her lap. Tori saw that Marilyn glanced away, unable to deal with how much their mother had aged.

'Hi, Mr Dix,' Tori greeted him. 'It's been a while. Nice to see you.'

Dix, concerned, said to the sisters, 'Nice to see you, too. Mom's kind of under the weather these days.'

Marilyn whispered angrily. 'She looks drugged and drunk.'

'Nah, you're imagining it.' He winked at them. 'Sometimes these places have more supplies than your local bar and drugstore.' He grinned. 'Just messin' with ya. You know, like you see in them old-time movies.'

He said to Helen, whose head was still down, 'Now, don't you get too excited, Mama, your girls are real glad to see you. So you have yourself a fun day.'

He winked and walked off.

Tori's eyes glistened. Her poor mom. She looked half dead.

A wispy little voice was heard. 'Is he gone, the stale cracker?'

Tori bent her head toward her mother. 'Mom? You mean your guard? He left the room.'

With that, the woman perked right up and cackled. 'Hate that cracker. Tricky Dix always wants to get into my whitey-tighties.'

Both daughters stared, startled.

Helen pretended embarrassment. 'Oops, he's the one wearing the whitey-tighties, or is it tighty-whities? I mean my pantaloons.'

Marilyn whirled her finger alongside her head, indicating: Mom was batty.

Tori looked straight at her mother. 'Do you know who I am?'

She grinned. 'Would I ever forget my baby? You were my "get up every morning Glory". 'Member I used to say that to you when you was an itty-bitty little thing? Morning Glory, up and at 'em.'

Her mom was hallucinating. She was in prison; her grandmother Ida was the one to wake her in the mornings. Before she left us. 'Yeah, sure I remember. But Mama, I want to be called Tori.'

Helen reached over, whispering. 'No, you're my Gloria.' She giggled and said softly, but dramatic-ally: 'You ready for your close-up, baby girl?' She pointed toward Marilyn. 'But who's that one over there?'

'It's Marilyn, Mom, your oldest daughter.'

'Oh, her. 'Member all those husbands? I liked the baseball player. The Blonde Bombshell never could keep a man.'

Marilyn shrugged. Tori shrugged back at her. She knew her mother was talking nonsense about her. As if she was that famous movie star.

Tori paused. 'You lost a lot of weight.'

Helen cackled again. 'Easy-peasy way to die. Oopsie-doopsie, I mean diet.'

She placed her still-clenched hands on the table. 'So how's them religious folks? Still dragging you to that phony-baloney TV minister? Got his God learnin's from his bible, Religion for Dummies?'

Both girls looked up sharply.

'So what's goin' on with Gerty-dirty and Maxel-axel?'

'They're just fine,' Tori whispered, choking on her lie. Then, unable to stop herself, 'Gertrude died—'

Helen interrupted. 'I knew it!' She broke into song, 'Ding Dong! The Witch Is Dead.'

The sisters were speechless.

Helen placed her finger to her lips. 'Gotta watch what ya say round here. Secret, everything's a secret. Specially round Tricky Dix, ya know.'

'Yeah, I'll be careful.' Humoring her. Tori started slowly, 'Mom, I need to go away.'

'You're ready. At last. You betcha, you get the hell out of Dallas. Wait, was that . . . Dodge?'

'Mom, I really need your advice.'

Marilyn shrugged again, a waste of time, asking a nutcase for advice.

Helen whispered, 'Go find Dad Dah. Your mamma's done living, so get you to Dad Dah.'

'You mean Dad? Are you talking about Dad?'

Marilyn couldn't stand it anymore. 'Why are you listening to this lunatic?'

Helen tossed Marilyn a nasty glance then turned to Tori and grinned. 'You always was my special late baby, born in a special way and a special time. You, always the smart one.'

Marilyn had enough. 'Yeah, Mom, you should talk about smart. Rob a bank and end up in here. Destroy everyone's lives.' She turned her back on her mother.

Helen reached across the table, pushing with her closed fists, forcing Tori's hands open. She indicated that Tori should lay her hands under hers. Tori did so. And, with incredible speed, the woman shoved something into her daughter's hands. Just as quickly, Tori immediately slid the crinkled paper down into her skirt pocket. 'It's a picture,' Helen whispered.

Helen upended her hands, now empty, 'Get thee out of here. Find Hah Hah and Lie Lie and Dad Dah.' She whispered, very softly, 'Go where the flamingos fly; shhh. The walls have ears.' Following that, she pounded on the table, singing loudly, 'Here Comes the Bride.'

Causing a disturbance that made other convicts in the room respond noisily, banging on their tables, singing the wedding song along with her. Which brought Dix hurrying back. He helped Helen out of her chair.

'I'm sleepy, Dix-ee. I need my nap.' She leaned into him, as if suddenly feeble.

The guard addressed the daughters, 'I need to take her back now. Sorry.'

'Bye, Momma,' Tori called out after her.

Her mother tossed her a sprightly, cheerful bye-bye wave, with her hand behind her back.

As they waited on the exit line, Marilyn commented, 'Well, that was a waste of time. Our mother is a mad woman. Dumb as a dodo bird.'

Tori smiled. 'I'd call it sly as a fox.' She managed a swift glimpse at the photo in her pocket, quickly glancing at the writing on the back.

'Come on, all that oopsie-poopsie and "Here Comes the Bride"? If that wasn't loony, then what was it all about?'

'It was all about me finding Dad.'

'What on earth are you talking about?'

'Our dad! The dad I never met. Isn't that cool?'

Marilyn gasped. 'You know damn well Dad died years ago in that flood. The day you were born. Are you nuts, too?'

'No, he didn't. Mom just told me. He's alive! And I know where he is.'

As they passed Dix, shepherding the visitors out, he winked and gave them a jolly salute. 'Bye, ladies,' and to Tori, 'Hope to see you again, real soon, good lookin'.'

Tori's mind was on the photo waiting for her in her skirt pocket. She didn't notice Dix pick up his cell phone. Nor did she hear him say to someone, 'Hey, Docks, You're not going to believe what I just heard. Take out the old shotguns and give 'em a spit and a polish. After all these years . . .'

60

Part Three
The Puzzling Present

Ten

The Washing-Machine Gang

Here we are once again, after quite a long time, piled into the cramped laundry room alongside the elevator on my floor. Sophie is first in line to do her dirty laundry in the one ancient, creaky washer. Bella will be next, once Sophie shifts the clean wet things into the single dryer. We have to help Sophie because her legs are getting worse. She describes herself in a world of pain, and was depending on her cane much more.

Evvie, Ida and I form a line and take turns helping her shove her clothes into the dilapidated machine. Evvie laughs. 'I think it's funny, our still having hush-hush meetings in the washing-machine room. Especially since it hardly fits two people in at a time. And that we could easily meet in one another's apartments. When did we start using it as our room for secret meetings?'

'I don't remember,' Bella says in her meek little voice. 'Anyway, I hardly remember anything anymore.'

Evvie adds, 'It must have been on a case we solved a long time ago.'

Bella jumps in. 'Yes. And we didn't want anyone hearing us talking. I think we were hiding from Hy. We're always hiding from Hy.'

Sophie chimes in with her complaint. 'Especially

since we can hardly breathe in here with the detergents and bleach and other awful damaging chemical fumes. And when will we ever get new machines? These things are dying on us.'

Evvie sighs. 'I bring it up in every board meeting and it always gets ignored.'

I wait for Ida to contribute her major kvetch about all the other things wrong with this space. No air. No room to turn around. Dim lighting. Damp. But the new, unimproved Ida is not herself these days.

'Ow!' Sophie screams. 'These damn legs.' She smacks her cane in protest, whacking the pock-marked wall, peeling away after so many years of steam.

'So sit down if it hurts so much.' Evvie indicates the one small rickety chair with its spindly thin arms.

'I can't sit down, because then I won't be able to get up. My knees don't work anymore.'

The washer goes into soak mode and the sucking noise makes us squirm. Sophie shouts to be heard. 'My life is hell. I'm afraid to sit down anywhere. What if I'm stuck on that seat forever?'

Bella tries to be helpful. 'Remember what the physical therapist suggested. Nose over toes. Nose over toes. Bend that far down and you can get up. Maybe.'

'Or fall on my head.'

'I thought you went to the neurologist yesterday.' This from Evvie.

'For more useless tests and X-ray results. Thank goodness for the little bit Medicaid pays. Yeah, that doc was some big help.'

64

Bella, not getting the sarcasm, vigorously shakes her head. 'No, he wasn't a help. Tell them. Tell them what that *momser* said.'

Sophie imitates the doctor's sarcastic tone. 'Nothing wrong with your legs. They're just old. Like you are. So live with it.'

Evvie says, 'Another biting letter to the AMA soon to be ignored.'

I frown. There are many doctors in Florida who have no sympathy with anyone aging. Wait until *they* get old.

I knock on the small, pitted table that holds our waiting clothes baskets. 'Okay, our meeting should come to order.' And the washer groans into wash cycle.

All eyes immediately flash over to Ida. This meeting is about her.

Evvie advises, 'Talk fast. When it goes into spin, we won't be able to hear ourselves think.'

First, we all help the worried Sophie into the one chair and everyone looks to me, forever assumed to be the person in charge.

'Ida, what's happening? Have you found out anything? Did Tori tell you anything?'

Ida stands straighter, arms hugging, as if for comfort. 'I don't see much of her. She stays up late working on her computer. When she wants to talk on her phone, she locks herself into the bathroom. In the mornings, she's up early, grabs one of her power bars and she's out the door. Gone for hours. I have no idea where she goes, or how she gets around. I ask her where she's been and she says "out". I ask where, out? She says "about".

'She always takes her computer and backpack. Yesterday she forgot it, or had someplace to go where she shouldn't bring it, who knows?'

Evvie says slyly, leading her on, 'And what did you do when you saw the backpack left behind?'

Ida cries out. 'Yes, I did just what you think I'd do. I paced my apartment back and forth, back and forth again, fighting with my conscience.'

Bella giggles. 'Your conscience lost.'

'I double-locked the front door in case she came back for it. I spied on my own grandchild. I'm so ashamed.' Ida's face reflects her feelings; circles around her eyes from lack of sleep, cheeks drawn in, skin sallow.

'And? And? Tell us already. What did you find out?' Sophie wagging her cane around as if it were a fly swatter.

Ida snuffles. 'There was a lot of money in a pouch. I was afraid to count it in case she came back fast. But I could tell there was a couple of hundred dollar bills!'

'Interesting,' says Evvie.

'Some more grungy clothes. She obviously didn't spend money on anything decent to wear. I also found an old map of Fort Lauderdale. Her cell phone was in there, which made me think she'd be back soon. It must have been new, because I've seen this kind advertised on TV and they are expensive. Of course I didn't know how to see what calls she made. And there's a postcard I sent her years ago. It was a picture of the beach and I'd written "Wish you were here".' She sighs. 'How flippant I was.

'Then I heard her at the door. Working the

double locks. I shoved everything back in and prayed I did it in the same order she left it.'

Evvie says, 'Good thinking.'

Bella tugs at Ida's gray pleated skirt. 'So, all right already, what happened?'

'I ran into the kitchen and grabbed some pots and things from the fridge, so she'd think I was cooking.'

Bella is delighted. 'That was so smart.' Bella is fond of that expression.

'Not that smart. If she'd paid attention, none of the items I pulled out made any sense. Peanut butter and two frying pans? But all she was interested in was her backpack. She looked at me suspiciously and I nearly died of fright.'

'Well,' I comment, 'it doesn't tell us too much. Either she was fond of your postcard or it was in there because of your address. The map doesn't help us if it's just her being a tourist. And why a map when the kids of today use the GPS on their phones to find places.'

Ida shrugs. 'One more thing. I've seen her clutching something she looks at sometimes. It wasn't in the backpack. She hides it somewhere. I could tell it's a photo.'

'Can you describe it?'

'I only got a quick look. I was afraid she'd see me.'

'Try to remember anything you can about it.'

Ida thinks. 'The photo is small, a black and white.'

'What else?'

She thinks. 'I only had seconds but I had the impression it was something taken at night, with very little light showing. Or maybe with a flash that didn't work. Wait! I remember something. It had some faded ink words on the back that I couldn't read.'

'Well done. That might help us one of these days.'

Suddenly, I'm aware of Ida crying. Not listening to me. 'Ida, what?'

Running her hands through her wash basket, twisting items in her fingers, 'I was remembering my little girl. My daughter, Helen. Always the dreamer. And when she married Fred Steiner, they were like two babes in the woods. No sense of reality, either of them. They went to the movies a lot. Saturday cheap matinées. They lived fantasy lives. They nicknamed themselves Helen Hayes and Fred Astaire, and believed life was a movie story promising happy endings. They even named their children after movie stars.' The sobs seem to catch in her throat. 'I failed her. And my beautiful grandchildren. I failed them all. God is punishing me for what I did to my family.'

Karumph! The washer goes into a whirling dervish of spin cycle and we all jump. And the mood is gone. Ida snaps out of her reverie.

We take turns with our washing and drying, exchanging gossip, useless observations and lots of frivolous maybes. Trying to take Ida's mind off her problem grandchild. Then, a brief interrupted moment of drama, when Bella realizes she's dropped a bright red blouse into a white wash, its colors instantly bled. Better that kind of bleeding than what's in my mysteries, and real life.

Laundry is done. With baskets of clean clothes, we head for the door. I'm about to turn out the light when I hear, 'Ouch! Help! Don't leave me. I knew this would happen! I'm stuck in this darn chair!'

We turn and face Sophie and indeed she is wedged in. While she whines, Evvie grabs one arm, I take the other, and we pull her out.

Bella chuckles and shakes a finger at her. 'You forgot. Nose to nose. Nose to nose.'

'That's nose to *toes*,' Evvie reminds her.

'Whatever.'

'Shut up,' says Sophie, in a lather of self-pity.

Surprisingly, Ida stops us at the door. 'Wait!' What's this? We turn and stare at her.

'If I had told you my pathetic story years ago, when I moved here, you would have had nothing to do with me.' Ida bends over, breathless, as if her body no longer has bones, as if there is nothing left inside her heart.

I am reminded of the few hints Ida gave me about her past when she first came to live here. But I realized there was so much she left out. I never pressed her for more.

For a few moments we stand there, surprised. We don't know what to say or do.

'If I tell you now, you'll hate me.'

Evvie says, 'Nonsense, nothing you can tell us will change how we love you.' We take turns reassuring Ida that we'd always stay friends.

I think about Tori. I was surprised at myself for my harsh feelings about her. But I felt that anyone who hurt my friends hurt me. And Tori was hurting Ida.

Now, maybe we'll find out why.

Ida faces us, her expression grim. It's about time I told you the truth. All of it. Every miserable bit of it.'

Eleven
Ida's Story

We are in Evvie's apartment. Our laundry baskets filled with clean clothes wait for us at her door. It was time to leave the crowded, claustrophobic laundry room. We need space to let Ida breathe. Evvie's apartment is a perfect choice. Everything she surrounds herself with reflects her positive attitude toward life. Bright-colored accessories, and of course, her favorite posters; with her love of movies and the theater. The ones that please me most are posters of Bette Davis in *All About Eve*, Katherine Hepburn in *Stage Door*, and the always wonderful Meryl Streep in *Sophie's Choice*. Leave it to my sister to be attracted to strong women's roles.

Evvie serves us all chamomile tea in an attempt to relax us. Especially Ida, but she is still shaky. She needs to talk and we need to listen.

We sip our tea, waiting for her to start. And fifteen minutes goes by.

Bella looks to me for guidance. She doesn't understand why no one is saying anything. I seat myself on the couch next to her and whisper in

70

her ear, 'Shh, Bella, Ida needs to tell us things, and they are very important.' I reach out and give her a quick peck on the cheek. Reassured, she scoots her body further back into the pillows, making herself comfortable.

She and Sophie share smiles as they reach for cookies to go with their tea.

Ida, standing up, suddenly looks at all of us, as if she'd been in a trance and just woken up. She pulls her shoulders back as if preparing her body for battle. Her words pour out, as fragile as her body. I get the feeling she's ready to spill her guts, and will be unable to stop herself. No matter how long it takes, we'll listen. We are glued to her words.

'Once upon a time,' Ida says with irony, 'there was a very happy family. My darling daughter, Helen, and her sweet, kind husband, Fred, and my two adorable grandchildren. They had bought one of the charming new tract houses over the hill from Los Angeles in a fast-growing area known as the San Fernando Valley. So Murray and I bought there as well; we moved in half a block away. The other grandparents, Fred's mom and dad, Max and Gertrude Steiner, did the same. Three blocks further. It was glorious, going back and forth in each other's houses. Holidays. Birthdays. So much laughter. So much joy. So much love. We all assumed we'd live happily ever after just a few doorways apart.'

Bella claps her hands. 'I love hearing stories, just like when I was a little girl and my mom took me to Saturday story-time in the library.'

Sophie throws a pillow at her. Evvie shoots her a dirty look. I put my finger on my lips. Everyone lets her know she should be quiet.

'Sorry,' she whispers, covering her mouth, telling us she got the message.

Ida is so into her story, she isn't aware of the interruption. 'Such good years. Year after year after year. We thought it would last forever.

'Then everything changed. The bubble burst. Banks failed. The whole neighborhood died. The country went downhill.'

Ida stops. Evvie refills Ida's cup of tea. Her friend's hands are shaking.

'Hard years. People out of work. Fred lost his job. Even Max and Murray were struggling in those difficult times. I had no idea what my daughter and son-in-law were up to. When I was with them, they put on a brave face.'

Bella leans forward. Sophie shifts her body around to get more comfortable.

'I found out that, in his desperation, Fred got in with some bad people and soon they were growing and selling marijuana. And, to everyone's shock, Helen became pregnant again. Later-in-life motherhood, with girls in their teens. That frightened me into worrying even more.'

My girls are hanging on Ida's every word.

Ida paces. We watch her, breathless, for moments, unable to say anything. She turns and faces us again. Her eyes, staring at nothing.

'I found out about the marijuana. I was terrified that they would get caught with the plants growing in their back yard. I begged them to

72

stop. It was against the law. They wouldn't listen. The money was keeping them alive.

'It was then I did something so stupid. I made the decision that changed all of our lives. I called the cops and reported them! Turned in my own children!'

Suddenly Sophie's hand shoots up. 'I need to go to the bathroom.' She gets the response she expects. *Now? When Ida is telling us this!* She sees it on all their faces.

Sophie gets up from her chair with the help of her cane.

As she hurries from the room she says, 'I'll be right back.'

The mood is broken. Bella gets up to stretch. Evvie joins her. I look at Ida. She stares back at me with tears in her eyes.

Sophie is as good as her word. She hurries back 'Sorry. Sorry.' And takes her seat again.

Ida turns back to us.

Evvie has to say something. She can't wait. 'Why would you do that?'

In agony, Ida responds, 'How many times have I asked myself the same question?

'I didn't think. I panicked. My daughter and her husband, so young, so naïve. So gullible. Who knew what kinds of people were giving them dangerous ideas? I wanted to tear those plants right out of their ground. With two children and one more coming, I thought them so foolish. I pleaded day and night. Give up that dangerous game. Things will get better. I promised.

'But I was the foolish one. I kept hearing horror stories of how dangerous drugs were. I called

73

the police, afraid that if the kids were caught at it, it would be worse for them. At the time, I assumed compassionate cops would slap their wrists and give them a warning. Just to teach them a lesson. And that they would go especially easy on them, with Helen being pregnant.

'I had no idea that my poor misguided children were way past marijuana; they had robbed a bank! Unbelievable – robbed a bank! How could that be? A major crime. The police hadn't known the identities of the couple who had robbed the bank, until my showing up conveniently revealed their names.'

Ida sobs, 'They chased after my pregnant daughter as if she was a dangerous criminal! Found her, arrested her! She gave birth to her baby in a prison cell! Then she was given up to twenty years in prison! My poor Helen.

'My fault. All my fault!'

She's shaking. I help her to a seat.

I ask what we must all be thinking, 'What about Fred?'

She can barely get the words out. 'He tried to escape, but they had been trapped in a rain culvert and it flooded and he drowned. They never found his body.'

The girls can hardly bear it, listening to Ida pour her heart out.

Ida, deep into her memories, goes on. 'So, there I was, riddled with guilt and, irony of ironies, Helen begged me to take care of all the children. Me. How could I refuse? How could I tell her, her own mother was the one who'd turned them in?

'Murray and I moved into Helen and Fred's once happy home. Once we realized that Helen would be away for years, we sold our house. Max and Gertrude promised to help, but they didn't. Fred's death changed them; made them shrivel up and retreat into themselves.

'I was not so young anymore. It was hard caring for two frightened and confused misbehaving teenage girls and a brand-new baby. A colicky baby who kept me up nights with her crying.

'Then Murray got sick. No, worse than that, it was terminal. Then I was sharing those sleepless nights not only with a crying baby, but tending to a husband slowly dying.

'When Murray died not long after, on a miserable stormy January day, I lost it.

'Immediately after the funeral, I called Gertrude and told her I was leaving and that she and Max were to take care of the children. I hung up, not giving her any chance of refusing.

'I ran away and had a nervous breakdown, fifty miles later. The doctors in my rehab hospital finally told me, after many painful months, that I was well enough and I should go back into the real world.

'Coward, that I was, I could never face that world again. I felt I had burned my bridges forever. And then, not knowing where else to go. Three thousand miles later, I showed up here.'

Ida stops, exhausted.

Her head is bowed. Ida is through talking.

I can't just sit there; I get up to hug my friend.

The girls instantly join me and we encircle Ida with our love.

Every one of us is sobbing.

Later that day, I try to tell Jack some of what transpired in that emotional morning. And I cry again. He wants to know why I'm crying. I can't explain it. I tell him I can't talk about it now; it hurts too much. He comforts me, lovingly, and doesn't try to press me. And then asks the question that's on all of our minds: 'Have you found out why Tori is here?'

I have only a partial answer. But not now, my darling, not now.

Twelve

Jack and Gladdy at Dinner

The next night, over a delicious favorite meal of Jack's – chicken fricassee, wild rice and steamed broccoli – I try to tell Jack what transpired in yesterday's tense event. 'Tried' is the operative word.

He asks, 'You spent all those hours in the laundry room? Wasn't that tiny room claustrophobic?'

'We moved out when the laundry was done and went over to Evvie's.'

'How did that work out, being that your sister is the Queen of Clutter?'

'It wasn't a problem. She'd had cleaned that morning. Ida unburdened herself—'

76

Jack interrupts me again, something unusual for him. 'Could you pass the ketchup?'

'Since when do you ever pour ketchup on your chicken? What's going on? Why are you side-tracking me?'

Jack leans back in his chair. 'Are you listening to yourself?'

'What does that mean – listening to myself? I assumed I was speaking and you were listening to me.'

'I have a question for you which will be worth twenty points on your scoreboard, if you're right.'

What is the matter with him; it's so not like him? 'What scoreboard? What points? What are you raving about?'

'That's my point. It's what *you're* talking about. Okay, here goes. What did we talk about at breakfast this morning? That's my question.'

I put down my knife and fork and hope my meal doesn't get cold. This chicken dish is one of those dishes that takes a lot of prep time. And should be eaten definitely very warm.

I think about what answer to give, regardless of how annoyed I am. 'Well, as usual, first I worked on my Sunday crossword puzzle.' About my puzzle. I always start it on Sunday, but it stays on the table all week long, until completed. 'I asked you for some answers that you might know, on subjects you excel in.' Politics, sports, crime, macho-male stuff. Smart guy, you helped me fill in some blanks.

He pretends to be a buzzer. Buzzing me – wrong.

'Not about the puzzle?'

'Nope.'

'Well, we did discuss the editorial page from that same Sunday paper.'

'Not even close.'

'Will this game stop before my chicken gets cold?'

'Up to you. Haven't given me the right answer yet. The puzzle and news page took only about fifteen minutes. Breakfast lasted for about forty minutes. What else did we talk about?'

I stop and eat bits of food, an act of rebellion. I want to make my point. Eat it warm and now.

'Okay, I'll give you a clue. When did Tori get here?'

Me, being petty, 'That's a different question.'

Jack takes a few bites to humor me. 'The answer to that side question is – less than a week ago. When you came home from your deli brunch that day, it was all about the new kid who'd showed up unexpectedly, and her odd response to Ida and that rather remarkable sentence tossed out about someone maybe who wants to kill her.

'Then we had the group afternoon session in Ida's apartment, with Tori doing her naked-I'm-gonna-shock-you tough-kid extravaganza.

'It was followed by that same evening, after dinner at our place, being barraged by the usual suspects and what was it about? Why, it was part two of the Tori and Ida show.

'I can do a day-by day breakdown of the same rigmarole, with the big after-laundry cry session, leading up to this very morning's breakfast. Do you get my drift?'

I am startled. He's right, he's absolutely right.

Tori and Ida and their war have been on all our minds since the girl showed up. We want to help Ida in some way. So, there's been a lot of discussion. But do I make that clear to my husband? No, I say, 'Jealous, are you?' A stupid response. The wrong comeback.

Silence. Then, from out of nowhere, Jack tosses at me 'What the heck is "fricassee"? Where did our chicken dish get its name from? I'd like to know why that particular chicken got that name.'

This is ridiculous. I answer, being huffy, 'Fricassee comes from the French, meaning cutting up the chicken, then you sauté it, finally you braise it and serve it in its own sauce.' So, there, okay?

'Thanks, that explains everything. Except, what is "sauté"?'

Now I'm answering fast and mean, 'Sauté is also French. Means dancing. Like the onions dancing in a hot pan of oil!'

'And, for now, the $64,000 question. So, what's "braise"?'

That does it. I get up ready to throw my half-eaten chicken fricassee at him. 'Hey, Chef Boyardee, what are you going on about? What's all this nonsense?'

Jack gets up, too. 'Just trying to show you that we are able to talk about subjects other than the Tori-Ida show. Didn't we just have a nice discussion about chicken?' He shrugs, pretending innocence.

He's funny. He's clever. He understands me. He's so protective of me. He cheers me up. He loves me. He's mine. I'm so lucky.

We move toward each other, meeting behind

the dining-room table. And we kiss. Do we ever kiss!

He whispers in my ear, after nibbling on my earlobe, 'You'll tell me all about it one of these days, not now when it hurts so much.'

Then, with a big smile he adds, 'Warm up the fricassee, honey. It's getting cold.'

Thirteen
Starbucks

Tori lines up everything she needs on a table originally meant for four, but luckily the Starbucks is fairly empty. No one is bothering her near the rear of the coffee shop, which gives her extra privacy. She has been careful coming to different coffee shops each time. Always on the lookout for that damn SUV and her now known enemy, Chaz Dix. Tori looks around again; the coast is clear and she is safe.

She smiles, thinking of Grandma Ida and her pals trying to guess what she's up to. None of their business. Grandma Ida gave up all rights to her when she abandoned her family years ago. Now it's up to her to save them all.

Down to business. Out of her backpack she retrieves, and notes: Ear buds. Check. iPhone. Check. Laptop. Check. Map of Broward County. Yes. And a large, steaming latte in front of her, proof that she has the right to use the store as her private office.

Of course she could do all her searching on her phone and computer, but the crumpled old map had originally been owned by her mother more than thirty years ago when she and her dad lived in Florida. Many things were circled on the map and they might be important.

The photo, the one that her mom had slipped to Tori, while singing the wedding song, of her then young parents seated with another young couple, is propped up on a menu in front of her. They were smiling for the camera; her parents' wedding day? Such a happy-looking couple. Shining with joy. This photo is her mother's hint? She squints at the back of the photo yet again. Even though the ink is practically invisible, with the small magnifying glass she bought, she's sure she read it right – *The Woodleys. Ft. Lauderdale.*

A few sips of the delicious latte and she's ready to roll.

Obviously this couple – first names unknown – were close friends. She is sure Hah Hah and Lie Lie is a clue, but if so, what does it mean? This photo is all she has to go on to find her father, and she is certain the Woodleys would know where he is. She works with this supposition – it's more than that; it's a huge hope – that this couple is still around, still alive, still lives here.

But is Woodley even a person's name? What if it was a street? A name of a place? A building, a park? *The Woodleys.* Quickly, with her fingers moving swiftly on the computer keys, she finds none of these names on a building, or restaurant, or even parks. Maybe years ago? She Googles every name for any possible historical reference. No match.

She feels sure they are people, not places. She will reference every Woodley family name in the county. But she worries. What if they no longer live in the county? Was she going to search through the entire state? And maybe they were no longer in Florida at all? She wouldn't let herself believe they were dead.

No, she is going with her heart. She feels her father is nearby. She laughs at her self-delusion. But it's all she has going for her.

So many Woodleys. Eight of them listed in the county phone book.

Grimly, she thinks, one by one, she will call or visit all of them.

She types out a list of her means of approach. As she copies and pastes and her latte grows cold, she silently practices her phone approach. Hello, my name is Tori Steiner. I'm looking for a couple named Woodley. No, I don't know their first names, but they would be about fifty. They lived in Fort Lauderdale in or around 1980 . . .

She is aware of something occurring at the counter behind her; is it some argument with the barista about their coffee? But, whatever, she doesn't want to be disturbed, or worse, involved. She ignores the ruckus.

She dials the first number. She hasn't passed reciting 'a couple named Woodley . . .' when

82

she hears a surly male voice 'Not interested!' Slam, bang hang-up!

The second call reaches a woman who must have been deaf. She keeps saying, 'I don't want any, whatever you're selling. Don't call me again! Damn politicians!' And then she, too, hangs up.

Tori is on her third disappointing call when she is aware that there are two policemen in the coffee shop. She is suddenly nervous.

One of them taps her on the shoulder. She takes the ear buds out. For a moment she panics. Do they know who she is? And how she left the Steiners? Have they been searching for her? Has she made a mistake and her past has caught up to her?

'Yes?' she asks, timidly.

He looks surprised. 'Weren't you aware that the coffee shop has just been robbed?'

Tori sighs, greatly relieved. It's not about her. She responds by pointing to her ear buds. 'No, no idea. I didn't hear anything.'

'You didn't happen to see anything? An elderly woman at the counter with a gun?'

She looks around. There's a small group of people milling about; police questioning them. The barista is waving his arms wildly.

Tori shrugs. 'I guess I was so busy . . . doing my homework . . . I didn't hear or see anything. Sorry.'

The policeman thanks her and walks back to the others, shaking his head.

Tori quickly gathers her belongings, shoving them into her backpack. Time to get out of here, she decides.

Fourteen
High Tea with a Lowly Thief

We have arrived. We get out of my old Chevy wagon and share a look of surprise. This is where Izzy, the infamous Grandpa Bandit, lives? Well, yeah, I guess so. This is the address he gave us. Once a fancy neighborhood, now fallen on not-such-good times. The house in front of us is one of the early mini-mansions of Fort Lauderdale.

Evvie wonders aloud, 'Is Izzy renting? Is Izzy actually an owner? Did Izzy buy it, maybe in foreclosure?'

Bella shakes her head. 'Don't start with "is he Izzy" stuff again. It gives me a headache.'

Sophie offers to translate. Like talking to a three-year-old. 'It goes like this. Your name is Bella. My name is Sophie. Grandpa Bandit's name is Izzy.'

'Oy, you did it again. Is this guy Izzy?'

We head for the front door. Ida has had enough. 'Forget it, already. Where's our housewarming gift?'

Bella rushes back to the car. 'I forgot.'

We all turn to look at her. 'Did it spill?' I ask with trepidation. Not a good idea for Bella to be in charge.

I see Sophie bending over the back seat, wiping

84

away water with tissues. 'Not too bad,' she mutters. She lifts our gift aloft.

'Is the goldfish still in the bowl?' I'm afraid to look.

'Alive and kicking,' she reports.

There had been a heated discussion on house-warming gifts earlier. Sophie wanted to know, 'What do you buy a crook for his housewarming? Handcuffs?'

Evvie couldn't resist. 'A set of lock picks?'

Sophie came up with another. 'A nice pair of running sneakers?'

I comment, 'I'm sure he'll be happy just to have us over.'

Bella tries to work this discussion out in her overcrowded, bewildered head.

Goldfish wins.

Ida, impatient as always, heads for the door and rings the bell. We hurry behind her. Sophie, of course, is being careful with our little gold passenger.

The heavy coat-of-arms-encrusted door opens. And the bantam-sized lord of the manor answers, cravat around his neck, wearing British tweed and carrying a martini.

'*Mesdames, entrez-vous,*' Izzy says with a French accent, sort of.

We walk in and are suitably impressed. High-ceilinged, beautiful entrée hall with round oak table in the center holding a huge bouquet of seasonal flowers. Doors leading to other rooms. A massive, impressive walnut staircase stands before us.

'Welcome, welcome,' cries out our host, 'what's this you are carrying?'

Bella, 'A special gift for you.' She hands him the fish bowl.

Sophie, 'We brought you a housewarming gift.'

Izzy bends over the fish bowl, waving his pinky finger over its rim. 'Kitchy-kitchy coo. Adorable. I always wanted *un poisson.*'

Bella, horrified, 'Our little fishie is not poisoned!'

Izzy looks at her, eyebrows raised. 'I certainly hope not.'

Bella, at her most confused, thanks him.

We shake our heads, no point in trying to explain Izzy to Bella. Or vice versa.

Izzy takes the fish bowl, indicates that they stay where they are. In a few moments, he returns, fish-bowl-less. He announces, 'Let me give you the grand tour.'

The girls can hardly wait. They gather round him, and follow eagerly.

Izzy skips from room to room, indicating with many flourishes. Though I notice a genteel shabbiness to the furniture. Downstairs, a massive tile-floored kitchen. Old-fashioned stove and fridge. A library room with walls of books that don't look as if they were ever read. Three separate bathrooms. Impressive. Upstairs, four bedrooms. Very fancy. Lots of silks and satins. The fabrics around the four-poster beds seem threadbare. Miles of oak polished floors. Three more bathrooms. All in all, a very large, impressive place.

The portraits on the walls look like lords and ladies of another era. I wonder if they came with the house. The girls are dying of curiosity (a rather unfortunate phrase). I'm about to ask the question on all their minds when Bella does a Bella. We have a name for it – we call it blurting, or hoof-in-mouth disease.

Says she, 'You must have robbed a hundred banks so you could buy this place.'

Evvie gently puts her hand over Bella's mouth. 'You forgot, dear, that Izzy gave all that bank money away to help elderly sick people in need.'

Ever so cheery, Izzy ignores the comments. He is busy pointing out this, pointing out that. The girls remain in drooling mode.

We think the tour is over, but Izzy says, 'Let me show you my back patio and then, over tea, I'll tell you all about the house. You're gonna get a kick out of my view.'

And what an unexpected view it is. There is a vacant lot between the house and the next street, which consists of many different stores. And to our distress there is a branch of SunTrust Bank right next to a Starbucks.

Izzy jumps up and down. 'A SunTrust bank almost in my back yard. One of my earliest conquests. Isn't that a hoot!'

Evvie takes on a lip-pursed schoolmarm look. 'Now, now. I thought you said you were retired.'

'I did. I did. I am. I am. I am retired. Cross my heart, and hope to die, I'll never rob another bank again. I swear every SunTrust is safe. First Citizen Bank is safe. Legacy is safe. So is B of A and PNC. As safe as a virgin in an all-male college dorm.' He smirks at his little joke.

'Good man,' I say, ignoring the joke.

He giggles, waving at the bank. 'Too bad. I

coulda walked back and forth from my yard to this one. I bet they'd remember me.'

For the grand finale, he shows us an old beat-up wooden mini-garage with its connected metal storage shed, explaining that in years gone by garages were built toward the rear of the house and had room for only one car. 'Wanna see my fancy car? It's an Edsel.' He points to the rear end of a large auto, sticking almost totally out of the narrow garage.

No interest. With a last, longing look back at SunTrust bank he sighs dramatically. 'Tea is being served.'

The elegant drawing room is where we will have our tea. Seated in eighteenth-century walnut Queen Anne wing chairs, with tapestry covering and matching footstools. One could almost imagine a butler showing up and serving us. Lovely.

Our goldfish (with goldfish food) now has its home on a lush white marble fireplace mantel. Our gift once again is appreciated by Izzy. Sophie suggests it's the perfect pet. 'Low maintenance.'

As our host pours tea for us, my curiosity takes me to a black-and-white photo atop an antique baby grand piano. It is of a man and a small boy.

Izzy sees me and frowns. 'That's me, and my son at age nine. Another failure in my life. I wasn't much good as a husband, or as a father. We no longer speak. Chaz moved to the West Coast to get as far away from his useless dad as he could.'

It's a painful subject so I drop it. Speaking of painful subjects, Sophie walks around the room trying to balance her tea and cookies. 'Sophie, why not sit down—?'

She interrupts me. 'I'm looking for a chair I can get out of.'

'Here we go again with your aches and pains.' Ida, without Tori, has reverted to her old cranky self.

Izzy helps Sophie into one of the Queen Anne armchairs. He puts a pillow behind her back and lifts her legs, gently placing them on the footstool. 'This should help. Are you in pain, a lot?' asks the guy who, in his past criminal days, knew much about old-age hurting.

Sophie nods, and would go on and on, with an endless list of complaints, so Ida doesn't let her start. 'Just drink your tea.'

Izzy asks Sophie, still interested, 'Have you thought about medical marijuana? Helps a lot of people.'

The girls look at Izzy with alarm. No millennials here. We are of the generation that is taken aback by drug usage. Sophie finally says, 'Thanks for your kind suggestion, but I really couldn't.'

Time for me to change the subject. 'So, Izzy, tell us about the house.'

'Surprise. I was born here. My parents owned this place. Yeah, those fancy-schmancy portraits are my ancestors. My pop was a high-class crook; he worked in the stock market. I got married, so my wife and child lived here, too. Then my parents died, and so did my marriage.

My wife dumped me. My son took off as soon as he could.'

Evvie is enthralled. 'You could have sold this house for a fortune. Maybe you still can. You didn't need to be a crook.'

Izzy's head hangs low. 'I had nothing in my life. Rich kid. Wasted years. Dealing with stocks and bonds bored me. I disappointed daddy-o. I quit trying to follow in his boring footsteps. I needed something that made me glad to get up in the morning. When I got older I found my happy hobby. Stealing do-re-mi to help old folks who needed surgery.'

Sophie adds, gushing, 'You were so good at it. Loved the plastic gun in the pastrami sandwiches.'

Izzy blushes, pleased with the compliment. He shrugs. 'Jail time reformed me finally, and now you're caught up. Here I am. I'm looking into another happy hobby.'

'You could raise goldfish,' Bella suggests with a goofy smile.

He smiles back. 'Enough about me. Let's eat.'

We enjoy our jasmine tea with clotted cream, little crust-less cheese sandwiches, scones with strawberry jam and for dessert, petit fours. And a small sip of dry sherry. A good time is had by all. He gives us each a goodbye pat and off we leave to go back home.

I sense something dangerous is staring us in the face; how could we ever guess what it is.

Fifteen
Dinner with my Son-in-Law, the Cop

We are having dinner at our favorite family-owned Greek restaurant in Margate, Jack, Morgan and I. Jack's son is known as Morrie, to us all. Jack had been a policeman in New York years ago, and his son followed in his police footsteps. I look at this young, handsome guy at forty and I can imagine what his father looked like at that age. As far as I'm concerned his dad is just as handsome today, the only difference is gray hair and years of experience becoming the wonderful senior he is.

Morrie is stationed at our local precinct. He is our go-to cop when Gladdy Gold and Associates have cases that need law enforcement backup. Besides, he's adorable and very kind to his mom-in-law. Since he is usually too busy to visit, this is our monthly planned get-together dinner for catch-up time. Occasionally crime gets in the way, but most times we manage to make our dinner dates.

Jack lets me do all the talking. He eats with relish; I jabber in between bites.

During the avgolemono Greek lemon soup, a favorite, I regale him with tales of tea with our reformed robber, Grandpa Bandit, aka Izzy; he, the lord of the manor, who promises never to rob another bank again.

With our horiatiki, Greek salad, and zatziki, cucumber yogurt dip, I fill him in on Ida's unexpected visitor, the angry grandchild, and how she has affected her. And of the girl's private forays around town in search of something, which information she refuses to share with anybody. And of some dangerous mystery men who might be after her.

I also include the wild adventure with the alligator in the bottom of the pool, which has Morrie shaking with laughter.

By the time we are digging into our moussaka, our delicious lamb and eggplant casserole, Morrie has dozens of questions to ask me. Through chuckles. 'An alligator at the bottom of the pool. Really?'

'Really.'

'Does reformed bank robber Izzy actually live in a mansion?'

'Yes.'

'Did you believe him when he said he was retired?'

'I hope so.'

'Is Ida all right?'

'Not her usual feisty self.'

Morrie shakes his head. 'That's quite some mystery around her grandchild. What do you know so far?'

I let Jack take over, he's better at compiling. Besides, he's through eating and my moussaka is getting cold.

Mr Papadopoulos, the owner, comes over to make sure we regular customers are happy. We are. We exchange pleasantries; learn Mr P. is to become a grandfather for the fifth time. We congratulate him.

When he leaves us to continue to enjoy our meal, Jack answers Morrie's questions.

Jack fills him in about the crime and what happened. 'What we know so far is that Ida caused her daughter, Helen, to end up with a long prison sentence. It's now about sixteen years; the woman is still incarcerated. And Ida was supposed to raise the three grandchildren, but she fled.'

I take over, allowing Jack to enjoy his baklava. 'Ida's three grandchildren were left to be raised by their other grandparents, which Ida now knows was a terrible mistake; apparently they were cruel. A horrible experience for the girls. What we don't know is why the youngest of the three, Gloria, who calls herself Tori, is now staying with Ida. It's not as if she just ran away from home to be with her other grandmother. She behaves as if she hates Ida. So why would she come to live with her? Doesn't make any sense.'

Jack stops to sip his retsina wine, and then recites his interpretation. 'Since Tori's been here, she wanders around town by herself, plays down the story of the alleged potential killers and is utterly unkind to Ida. She seems to have plenty of money. Who, or what, she's looking for, or if she's even looking for anything or anyone, we have no idea. We don't know why she is here.'

I add, 'Nor do we know how long she is staying.'

Morrie muses, 'Go back to the part about the potential killers. We might assume she met up with them before she left LA or somewhere on her way to Florida. Anything that might give you a clue?'

I shake my head. 'She hasn't talked about why she left LA. As for on the road, the only town she mentioned staying over was La Mesa in New Mexico. That was about two weeks ago. She apparently met a number of men there. Wait a minute; she mentioned being upset that some of them had tattoos. Then again, tattoos are fairly common these days.'

Morrie leans back in his chair, content with his meal. 'Quite a story.'

'Enough about our little excitement, what's happening in your life?' I ask.

Morrie raises his hands as if to push the question away. 'Now, now, Mama Gladdy, my personal life remains personal.'

I pretend innocence. 'Would I pry? Would I ask if there's someone special in your life? Not I.'

Jack and Morrie both laugh. I am guilty of wanting him to find some lovely person and settle down. It hasn't happened yet. Jack changes the subject. 'Anything new down at the station?'

'Same old. Same old. Wife-beaters. Breakings and enterings, drive-by shootings.' Morrie is teasing, because we are lucky to be in a relatively safe area. 'However,' he says, 'something is new. There have been recent hold-up robberies at various Starbucks coffee shops. Of all places. Witnesses swear the crime is carried out by a little old lady. So, get this, now we have a Grand*ma* Bandit. How about that?' He grins.

Suddenly, I get this cold draft down my neck. Our Grandpa Bandit's words come back to me. 'I swear I'll never rob another bank again. I swear. But I am looking into a new hobby.' My mind flashes on Izzy's back yard. What was that place next to the SunTrust bank in the street below where he lived? Next to the bank where he would no longer rob again? A Starbucks, that's what. Could it be? Izzy in drag? He likes dressing up in costumes. That little devil.

Jack looks at me, puzzled. 'Something wrong with your food?'

I shake my head. But my mind is no longer on my dessert. Something clicks. I am pretty sure Gladdy Gold and Associates have a new crime to solve.

Part Four
The Past Revealed

Sixteen
Tori Story – Bye-Bye Baby

One week before

'Well, that's that.' The three sisters were standing outside the Steiner house. Tori handed Marilyn the key to the front door. Tori was dressed for travel, her style: tee shirt, shorts, Dodgers baseball cap, sneakers and backpack. Being Los Angeles, the weather was fine.

'I can't believe you found all that money around the house.' Marilyn was in awe.

'Yeah, mostly stuck in pages of thirty-year-old *Reader's Digests*. Also dug some of it out of flour canisters along with disgusting weevil bugs. Yuk. Even picked up a few hundreds taped behind the toilet seat tanks. I doubt if I discovered all of it. You might do some searching, yourself.'

That excited Shirley. 'I'm game for looking. I bet you didn't look between the mattresses.'

Tori shakes her head. 'Unbelievable. All that hidden money and we were living on food stamps. Hardly ever money for me to buy lunch at school. Crazy people.

Marilyn agrees. 'I guess now we'll never know why.'

'So, you got my story straight? I don't want the

cops looking for a runaway. But unless someone asks, don't volunteer anything.'

Marilyn recited, 'The story is: You're going to live with our grandmother, Ida. Even though all her mail came from Fort Lauderdale, lie and say she lives in Miami. I hope nobody questions the fact we have never been in touch with her since she ran off and left us.'

Marilyn. 'Your secret will be safe with me.'

'I don't ever intend to be anywhere near Grandma Ida, unless something goes wrong. I prefer that no one knows where I'm going.' She poked her fist in Shirley's stomach. 'And make sure you keep your mouth shut.'

Shirley pulled away, rubbing the hurt belly. 'I said I wouldn't tell. Stop hitting me!'

'You're the weak link. I don't trust you.'

'They can tear my hair out, pull my teeth out, I still won't tell. I swear! And what's a weak link?'

Marilyn shook her head. 'What *they* are you talking about?'

Shirley shrugged. 'Any old *they*. Cops? And what's the big secret anyway? Are you really going to Florida?'

Marilyn and Tori exchanged glances. Shirley, who was known for having a big mouth, should never be expected to keep a secret.

Tori glares at Shirley. 'Get this through your head. I'm not going to Florida, I'm going to New Jersey. I was just making that up. Got it? Got it!'

'Stop yelling. I got it. Okay, you're going to New Jersey.'

Marilyn handed Shirley the house key. 'Here. Go inside and look for some money. Grab some more dishes. Go shopping!'

Shirley grinned, her greedy eyes twinkling, grabbed the key and unlocked the door. 'Yay. Better than Walmart,' she called out at them.

They waited until she was out of hearing and sight.

'What a numbskull,' Marilyn commented.

The two sisters sat down on the doorstep. 'So aren't you going to tell me how you'll get there? Are you going to fly? You've got enough money.'

'I haven't decided. I've never seen any of the country, and I've never been on my own before. Maybe I'll hitchhike. Don't even start – skip the warning about hitchhiking. It might be fun. Or I'll catch a bus. Or fly later, somewhere along the way. As for you, go to a lawyer. I gave you all their papers. You should make a few bucks on this dump of a house. Their car is a joke. I suggest hiring a cleaning crew. Maybe dynamite would do a better job.'

'Never mind worrying about me. Are you sure you aren't going on a wild-goose chase? I listened to Mom's jabbering, but she didn't make any sense.'

'She did to me. The photo was taken on their wedding day so she sang "Here Comes the Bride". To tell me that. On the back of the card someone wrote The Woodleys, Ft. Lauderdale.'

'What the hell was Hah Hah and Lie Lie?'

'There were two couples in the photo. I remember long ago, in another prison visit, she told me about the good friends that were their

101

witnesses at their wedding. She told me they lived in Fort Lauderdale. She knew I'd put it together. But I don't remember their first names.'

'Wow. I never got any of that. But I still don't understand how you could believe Dad was alive.'

'When I was very little, before Grandma Ida ran away, we visited Mom, and Mom told me a story.

'Grandma Ida was furious with her for making up such a fairy tale. And she and Mom had a terrible fight. But Mom knew I'd believe it and remember it. About a mommy and daddy who loved each other and said if anything bad happened, and they got separated, the little girl in the story was to grow up and find her daddy. Her daddy would wait for her forever. In a place with a lot of palm trees.' She paused, saddened. 'Grandma Ida left us right after that visit.'

'Yippee!' Shirley was back outside again, announcing that her arms were filled with all kinds of good stuff, kicking a box with her feet. 'Got a load of great things. I'll never have to buy a dish or pot again.'

Tori shrugged. 'Better spray everything with disinfectant before you take any of that crap into your house.'

'Let's go, already,' she called, kicking her box down towards Marilyn's car.

The two sisters got up. 'Don't you want me to drive you somewhere? Anywhere?'

Tori shook her head.

'Good luck,' Marilyn said tearfully, 'and let me know what happens. I really do love you.'

'I will. But I'm sure it won't be for a while. I love you, too.'

They hugged, clutching one another, tightly.

'Come on, already,' Shirley whined, leaning her body against the car door to keep her box of treasures safe.

Marilyn walked toward her. 'Say goodbye, stupid.'

Shirley twisted her neck to see, calling out to Tori. 'Goodbye stupid.'

Marilyn smacked her on her head.

'What? What's that for?'

Tori waved as Marilyn drove away. And now for her adventure

Seventeen
Tori's Story – On the Road

Three days before

Tori climbed down out of the cab of the beat-up green truck. That is, she guessed it must have been green years ago. Now it was a scratched metal mess brought on by hot weather and desert sand.

'*Adios, Señor, muchas gracias,*' she said looking back up at the elderly Mexican farmer who had brought her along the last thirty miles without his speaking a word of English, with her trying out her high school Spanish. She hoped her goodbye was 'Tex-Mex talk,' given that her road trip on the I-10 was taking her deep south along the Mexican border.

The farmer drove away, turning his truck up the dirt road next to where he let her off.

Tori hand-brushed her clothes, as best she could, to get rid of straw that had filled the truck's front seat, as well as in back where the pigs were riding. She sniffed herself, hoping she didn't smell too much like pig, given that she had slept in a barn with them last night. She grinned. She loved her first road trip ever. She was having a wonderful time. Mile after mile, her dismal memories of Grandma and Grandpa Steiner were fading away.

She looked at the sign up ahead: 22 miles to La Mesa, New Mexico, population 728. She had taken a bus from LA to Phoenix, Arizona, then decided on hitching for a while. She'd already covered about 300 miles. So far, nice folks had given her rides, including Farmer Nuñez. Maybe, when she got to New Orleans, she'd fly the rest of the way. It would have been nice to stop at famous places like the Grand Canyon or maybe Carlsbad Caverns, but she had a purpose pushing her on. Florida would get her to her dad, she was sure.

Now, she wanted to get to La Mesa, find a motel and take a shower. Whew, those pigs had been smelly.

Her thumb went out and she settled down to wait. Hopefully not too long, since it was noon and plenty hot. She sat on a rock on the edge of the road, sucked whatever little water was still in her canteen. Her shorts were sticking to her body, and she was wondering what she might do if she didn't get picked up soon. There was no shade anywhere.

Just when she thought she could die here in this sauna, and panic was beginning to set in, thankfully, something was slowing down. She jumped up, waving wildly. It was a bus. Certainly not from any transportation company. It reminded her of photos of buses left over from the hippie 1960s. Playful cartoon drawings covered the sides, in bright paint colors, of guitars, horns and keyboards and some kind of name: BAND OF L-BROS, whatever that meant.

The door opened and a guy came out. She quickly summed him up: twenties, tall, skinny, dirty blond hair, straggly beard, jeans, tee shirt, and cowboy boots. Definitely cute. 'Hi, there,' he said to her, 'you look about ready to melt.'

'Have you got air-conditioning?' she gasped.

'Sure do. And a lot of hot air as well.' He grinned. A joke.

'So, what's with the name? You musicians?' Tori pointed to the drawings on the bus.

'That's us, we're a country band. We're the L-Bros. Four brothers with L names. I'm Luke. Inside, with their noses pressed against the glass, that there's Lonny, Larry and Lubbock.'

'Lubbock?'

'The accidental result of a night of too much boozing by Ma and Pa. They were in Lubbock, Texas, at the time.'

She glanced up at the front windshield to see three young guys who resembled Luke making silly faces and waving at her. She waved back.

'The dumb-looking one on the left is Lubbock.'

'I need a lift,' she said. 'Desperately, before I die of the heat.'

'Well, we can do light lifting.'

Both smiled at his humor.

'I was hoping for a ride to La Mesa.'

'No *problema*, we're on our way there, too. Got a gig tonight at the Hotel del Frontera.'

Suddenly they were aware of a car careening toward them at full speed. A black SUV. Coming to a full stop behind the bus. Two guys jumped out.

Again Tori did her quickie review. Older guys, forties maybe fifties. City guys, black suits, city clothes. Maybe businessmen or tough guys. Someone else behind the wheel. She couldn't see him through all the tinted plate glass.

One of the men spoke. 'We saw you from back there. Figured you needed a ride. Be glad to drive you wherever you want.'

'Thanks, I think maybe I already have a ride.'

Luke said, 'We offer beer and sandwiches.' He winked at her.

The men, confused, looked at one another. The talking man tried a suggestion. 'We have champagne. Chilled.'

Tori jumped up in glee. 'This is fun. Do I hear any other offers?

Luke was enjoying her game. He pointed. 'Looka da tope guys.'

She nodded, knowing the teen code for clueless and totally dopey.

Luke air-kissed her. 'We have music. We even write our own songs. L-Bros will keep you cool, fed and entertained.'

The city men exchanged baffled looks. The talker opened the car door and had a brief conversation with the unseen driver. He shrugged, turned back and said, 'We have satellite radio . . .?'

Tori and Luke burst out giggling. She raised her finger and pointed it back and forth at each them. 'Eeenie, meenie, minee mo.'

The SUV men didn't know what to say or do.

With that, she handed Luke her backpack, then jumped into the bus. Luke called out to the two men, '*Hasta la vista*, fellas.' Hopped on, and shut the door behind him.

The bus took off with Tori and the L-Bros, laughing.

Was she imagining it? She thought she heard someone shout 'Tori.'

Eighteen

Tori's Story – The Boys in the Band that Night

Tori had never known such happiness. Here she was seated in the comfy lounge of the Hotel del Frontera. The lounge and lobby, striking in dark paneled wood, were filled with Mexican art, paintings of early twentieth-century Western and Mexican scenes. She people-watched with delight. The men wore mostly white shirts and white pants and the women wore flared cotton skirts and off-the-shoulder embroidered blouses in bright colors. Both men and women wore cowboy boots.

Sipping a Coke, she listened to her new best friends onstage. All four L-Bros played different-size guitars and Luke was lead singer. Right now they were singing a song they wrote, called 'Riding on the I-10', about a lonesome cowboy who wanted to go home again, but he's not sure his wife will let him in. The only one who seemed to love him was his faithful dog, Moe.

The guys were fun to be with. They'd helped her check into a room in the closest motel, the same one the boys were staying at, the Frontera being much too expensive. She would have figured out how by herself, but they made it easy for her. Lots of teasing that she was welcome to share their rooms. They were just being playful. They took her out to a Mexican dinner. She got to eat the best, greasiest burrito con carne ever. When they brought her a beer she started to object. 'Hey, I'm still a kid.' But it turned out to be fake beer, non-alcoholic, a brand called O'Doul's. It was cold and delicious.

She was finally out in the real world and she loved it.

The evening spun around all too fast. She wished it would never end. The boys played one set after another and sat with her when they had breaks. Couples danced to their songs. It was a dance she'd never seen on *Dancing with the Stars* on TV. Lonny told her it was line dancing.

When they quit playing at one a.m., they

chatted as they walked her to her door. Luke informed her they were leaving early tomorrow for their next gig in Houston.

Larry said, 'Hey, girl, how about you stay with us and ride on as our groupie.'

Lonny added mournfully, 'We only got one groupie so far.'

'What's a groupie do?' She had heard the word and had a feeling she knew what it meant. Not good. Drugs, liquor and sex came to mind. She'd led a sheltered life, but she read a lot, plus TV; these were her education.

Lubbock chimed in, 'You go everywhere we go and your job is to sit in the audience and applaud us real hard and generally adore us.'

Lonnie added, 'And then there's the sex . . .'

Luke clapped his hand over his brother's mouth. 'Never mind, clam up.'

The brothers laughed.

Luke took her hand and walked Tori to her room, which was two doors from theirs. 'Ignore him. Lonnie's got a big mouth. He's just messin' with you.'

She took her key out and he put his hand over hers. 'How about we have a nightcap in your room together? Soft drinks, of course.'

Tori shook her head. She teased, 'I'm jailbait. I'm only fifteen.'

'I coulda swore you were eighteen,' he also teased. 'You coulda lied about your age.'

Shocked, 'No, I couldn't.'

'Of course you couldn't.'

She started to open the door. The room was dark. 'I could still tuck you in.'

109

She was sorely tempted, but she knew better. 'Nice try, but nope.'

'Okay, I'll settle for breakfast. Early, around six a.m. And if you want to ride along with us to Houston, that's good, too.'

'That's a deal. Breakfast and the ride. Count me in.'

He gave her a quick kiss on the cheek and walked off, whistling.

Tori entered her room smiling.

The smile faded as someone shoved her and knocked her off her feet.

The light was turned on and she looked up from the floor to see a face she knew. 'Hi, sweets, we meet again. I told you we would.'

Nineteen

Tori's Story – The Guys in the SUV

Tori stared in disbelief. 'Mr Dix, what the hell?'

'Yeah, it's me, your ma's very own special prison guard,' he said, pulling her up from the floor.

Tori stared at the two other men. She recognized them as the ones who came out of the SUV, offering champagne and satellite radio. It was funny then. Not funny now.

She glanced around her room. Her backpack had been tossed, and everything in it dumped on her bed. One of the guys was sprawled amidst her belongings. The other one now leaned against the door, arms folded. They'd seemed kind of rough outside, but here they looked downright dangerous.

'So, Dix, you were the one behind the wheel of the SUV.'

'That were me, chickadee.'

'What are you doing in my room? What are you doing here at all?'

'Don't hafta scrunch up your pretty forehead. I'll fill you in.'

Tori's mind was racing a mile a minute. Whatever was going down was trouble. How was she going to get out of this? She needed to run. But how?

She guessed Dix was going to do most of the talking.

Dix nodded and one of his men searched her. She squirmed and cursed, but he patted her down. Good thing she thought to hide the photo in her shoe this time.

The guys nodded back. She was clean.

'Might as well sit yourself down. It's gonna be a while.'

Tori tried to figure out what might help her, but there was nothing in sight she could use as a weapon. No use throwing a towel at him or the bible from the nightstand. She hadn't noticed it before, but just about everything else in the room was nailed down. The TV. The bedside lamps. Even the small night tables were bolted to the floor. Was management really worried about those crappy things being stolen?

Dix waited patiently. She sure as hell wasn't going to sit on the bed near that creep. She sat down slowly on the only chair in the room, a rocker with wagon wheels for arms.

'There, that's nice, make yourself comfy.'

He bent close to her, in her face. 'Good thing your cowboy pal didn't come in, he'd be DOA by now.' The two partners laughed. 'I'm gonna tell you a story. But first let me intro my buddies. The guy sittin' on your stuff is Hicks. The fella mindin' the door is Dockson. We've been buddies since we was babies. Show the girl our tats.'

Each of the three men lifted their shirtsleeves to show their tat inkings: Hickory, Dickory, Doc. 'Get it? Hicks, Dix and Dockson.'

'Yeah, cool.' Tori rolled her eyes. What the hell was going on?

Hicks said, 'See, this here in my lap is a gun, at the end of the gun is a silencer. Nobody'd hear a thing. And my pals have their guns as well.'

She was scared. No, terrified was more like it. She mustn't let them see her fright. Summoning up a bravado she didn't feel, she said calmly, 'Go ahead, Dix, start talking. Why aren't you in LA, where you belong?'

Dix took his time lighting a cigarette. 'It's all your fault, chickadee. Nowhere I'd rather be than back home, but you screwed up my life. I grew up in Florida. I hated Florida and because of you, I'm going back.'

Dockson grins 'And that makes him as mad as a hen with her feathers on fire.'

Tori tried not to show her fear. Florida, oh, God . . . what did they know?

The guys nodded solemnly in agreement, as if they were aware of how much their pal hated going back to his hometown. Dockson smirked. 'Dix comes from a family of crooks.'

Hicks added, grinning, 'Yeah, he comes by his trade honestly.'

Dix acknowledged their comments by smiling, waving them off. He reached down next to the bed for an open liquor bottle. He gulped some and passed it around, the bottle eagerly accepted.

Dockson, at the door, was restless. 'Get on with it, already.'

'What's your hurry? We want our girl to understand background, here. So, maybe she'll give us what we need willingly.'

Dix lifted her chin and smiled down at her. 'Back, fifteen or so years ago, five people robbed a bank. We had a perfect plan. We used two getaway cars. Us three guys raced outa the bank and jumped into our Jeep. Our other two partners, a husband and his very pregnant wife, were in the second car with all the money.'

Tori shuddered. Oh, my God! There were five of them? She never knew.

'See, if the cops stopped us, we were just guys out for an innocent drive. No cops would think of stopping a car with a pregnant woman, maybe on her way to the hospital. They were holding all our money, every hard-earned stolen buck, in their car. Any of this sounding familiar to you?'

Dix walked behind her and rocked the chair, slowly. Tori grew rigid, gripping the arms, trying to keep it steady. Leaning over her shoulder, he

113

said, 'Funny-lookin' rocker with wagon wheels. Never saw one like it before.' He rocked harder. Tori tried to keep her panic down.

Dockson chimed in. 'Two hundred thousand smackeroos, supposed to be safe in your daddy's wagon. We was gonna split the dough at our meeting place.'

Hicks added, 'But what the hell were they doin' down in the LA River wash?'

Dix shrugged. 'Easy, boys, remember the pourin' rainstorm that day. That's what your pretty ma told us. Runoff from the storm caught them in a flood, she said with the tears runnin' down that darlin' face. And they were trapped. They ran for their lives, so she said, leavin' all that money behind. And your poor dad fell and was sucked away downriver, along with the car and all the dough. Your mom was saved. Caught by the cops, with her ready to pop you out. And yeah, you did, right then and there in the jailhouse.'

All she could think – they had partners. How come Mom never told her about partners?

He rocked her harder. She was getting nauseous. She felt the fake beer gurgling in her stomach.

'But now that we know about dear old dad, something that always bothered me makes sense. When the cops found the car, there was only a couple of hundred soaking-wet bills in it. Everyone assumed the rest floated away. Yeah, sure. Floated away in a bag with Dad in Florida. All these years, living it up off our dough.

'Of course I didn't believe your mama. I managed to get guard duty in her cell block. No matter how many times I beat her up, she stuck to her story. I gotta give her credit, she never once turned us in to the cops.'

'Too bad she didn't,' Tori lashed out. 'They might have given my mom a lighter sentence. And then you wouldn't be her jailer, you'd be in your own little cell where you belong.'

'Water under the bridge, chickadee. Under the bridge.'

'I hate you!'

'Big deal. Everybody does. Get in line.'

Another slug of whiskey and more story. 'Imagine how mad we was. Even had a funeral for Daddy, of course, without the body. I didn't believe he was dead. Finally, after a lot of years, we had to believe Mom. Fifteen years, no matter what beatings or what drugs I pumped into her, no matter what threats, not a peep – until you. The baby born in jail, now growed up and old enough for her mom's secret to be let out.'

Tori wanted to jump off the rocker and beat him to death, but that was wishful thinking. 'You hurt my mama, you piece of garbage.'

Dix's partners pretended righteous indignation. 'She had no right to lie to us,' said Hicks. 'He's been livin' all these years and we never guessed,' whined Dockson.

Dix put his hands around her neck. 'Imagine my surprise when you and your sis came to visit and Mom gave you her crazy clues and I heard you say on the way out, you was going to find Daddy. Daddy, that sly old SOB, alive and well with all our money.'

'Yeah, spendin' our money,' chorused Dockson and Hicks.

Tori tried to calm her trembling body. She shook his hands off her neck. He laughed. She didn't know for sure how dangerous these men were, but she felt she needed to keep talking. 'Hey, Dix, how did you find me?'

'*No problema.* You disappeared. We guessed you left to find Daddy. So we visited your dopey sister. The chubby one, Shirley. She took one look at us, and our guns, and she vomited out words. What a nutcase; we couldn't shut her up. She kept yelling we shouldn't tear her hair out or pull her teeth out, and when I asked her where you were going she kept yelling, New Jersey, no, Florida, no, New Jersey, no, Florida.

'We finally figured out you were hitching rides. Clever girl, you, traveling the shortest route, the I-10. At first we planned on going to your granny in Fort Lauderdale to wait till you got there. But then, not sure you was going straight there, we wanted to see if we could find you on the road. We got lucky. It took us a while, going from town to town showing your photo. We could tell where you stopped. Places you ate. Places you slept. We caught up to you. We spotted you talking to the bus guys. We was barreling down to grab you but that damn ugly bus kid beat us to it.' He removed his hands and stretched. 'I think that catches you up, chickadee.'

He took another long slug of the booze, and shared it with his buddies. The bottle was empty and he pulled another one off the floor.

'Where's your daddy?' asked Hicks, waving his gun wildly.

No use denying the truth of what Dix said. But this was her truth. 'I don't know.'

Dockson taking his turn again, 'Yeah, sure, heading maybe three thousand miles across country and don't know where you're going?'

'All I know is that he's in Florida. Mom didn't know where.'

'But you had a clue, didn't you? You knew exactly what city to go to and it wasn't just to visit your granny.'

'Damn it,' Dix took over again. 'We're gonna have to do this the hard way. Let's look at all the clues in the little lady's backpack. Everybody settle down. It's gonna be a long night.'

Tori shivered. A long night, guys with guns who were getting drunk. With a wry smile, she hoped they didn't tear her hair out or pull out her teeth.

Twenty

Tori's Story – By the Dawn's Early Light

She had never felt so tired. Her eyes drooped, unable to keep her lids open. Every time her head dropped, desperate for sleep, he'd pull it back up. Dix took some pills early on, she guessed in order to stay awake. Hicks was snoring on the bed. Dockson, at the door, had

117

slid to the floor, occasionally dragging himself awake.

Dix stayed bright-eyed and bushy-tailed, whatever that silly saying meant.

'Okay, let's go over this again.' He pointed at the money pouch he had taken out of her backpack.

Again? Was it the fifth or fiftieth time? She had no idea how many hours had gone by. She wondered what time it was. The shades had been drawn before she'd even entered the room. She had left them open, earlier, but she hadn't paid attention when Luke brought her back to the room. Luke – would she ever see him again?

'Yes, I stole the money from my grandparents. They were dead, it didn't matter.'

'And the postcard from your grandma in Florida?'

'Yes, it's my grandma's address. I wanted to visit her.'

'You never, ever had any contact with her before? So why now? That's because she knows where your dad is.'

'Ask me fifty more times, the answer is the same. I'm sure she has no idea where he is. She has no clue I'm coming to Florida. I had no family any more. My other grandparents are dead. I wanted to move in with Grandma Ida.'

All Tori could think about was the photo she carried with her. Thank goodness she hadn't left it in her backpack, or even jeans. It was the only real clue she had toward finding her Dad, and she'd tear it up and eat it before she'd let that rat see it.

She tried to tune him out. Bla-bla-bla. He walked over to her and smacked her. 'Yeah, sure, moving to Florida. Liar! I'm talking to you, girly, so pay attention!'

Ouch, that hurt. Damn him, she thought, damn him. She wanted so badly to hit him back. But she had to stay calm. 'When are you gonna quit the pesterin'? My answers aren't gonna change.'

'You expect me to believe you just was poppin' down to Florida and, maybe, hope to run into him sometime?'

'I didn't know what I was going to do. Or how I'd find him. I just believed he was in Florida someplace. Maybe my mom is so crazy, she made it up. Maybe I'll never find him. Maybe he doesn't live there any longer. Maybe he's dead, and Mom wouldn't have known. Enough! Can I get some sleep, please?'

'I think you're trying to fool your pal Dix. So let's stop pretending the nonsense of visiting Granny. You are gonna find Daddy somehow.'

Tori refused to say anymore.

'So help me out here, little sweet pea. What do we do next? Stay glued to you all the way to Florida until you find him?'

Tori tried hard on a last futile attempt. 'I think you should go back home. This is probably a dumb thing I'm doing, but it was an excuse to get out of LA. See, you hate Florida and I hate LA. So you go back. And I'll try to make a new life on the East Coast.'

'Nice try, chickadee. You are one smart kid and my money's on you to find him. That's funny. It is my money that's on you to find.'

'Ha-ha, yeah, funny.'

'Trouble is, I think you are keeping something from me. Something you aren't sharing with your pal Dix.'

She wanted to wiggle her feet in her shoes, just to feel the photo, but she didn't dare give it away.

Tap-tap. A knock on the door.

Hicks's eyes popped open. Dockson looked confused. Everyone froze.

It was Luke, calling. 'Hey, sleepyhead, we gotta get going.'

Tori looked to the door, hope rising.

Dix grabbed her and, once again, his hands were around her neck. 'Easy, girl.'

Luke knocked harder. Hicks and Dockson were starting to drag themselves up.

Dix whispered in her ear. 'You tell him you're tired and need to rest some more.' He squeezed her arm and she tried to shake him off.

'I can't go with you,' she called out. With that, she elbowed Dix in the ribs, and jumped off the rocker. She ran to the door, tripping over the slow-moving Dockson. 'Help! Help!'

Luke yelled, 'Tori, get away from the door!'

She shifted her body just as two shots rang out, and the door lock was blown off; bits of pieces of wood dropped into the room. Seconds later, the door was shoved open, pushing Dockson out of their way; and there they were, the Four Musketeers, the L-Bros with four guns drawn.

Hicks groped all over the bed trying to find his gun. Dockson reached for *his* gun, but not in time.

'Stop, don't move,' Luke shouted, 'stop or I'll shoot!' He grinned at Tori. 'I always wanted to say that line.'

She ran to him and hugged him around his waist. 'My hero. I always wanted to say *that* line.'

Dix and pals remained rigid, not daring to move.

Lonny walked over and grabbed the gun off the bedspread, where it lay too far for Hicks to reach.

'How did you know I was in trouble?' Tori asked.

Luke smiled. 'The dumbos parked the SUV in front of your room.' He pointed to Hicks. 'Besides, earlier I saw the odd word "Hickory" on that one's arm. I saw a gang tag also. I knew these guys were up to no good. We decided not to wait till breakfast time. It's three a.m.'

Lubbock added, 'The minute you said you couldn't come with us, we knew for sure you were in deep . . . well, you know what.'

Larry jumped in. 'We knew you wouldn't want to miss a free breakfast and a free ride.'

Again from Luke. 'Besides, you yelled "help".' The brothers laughed.

Larry asked Luke, 'What do we do now?'

Dix stood in front of them, arms folded, arrogant. 'Yeah, kids, what now? Really gonna shoot us?'

'Nah, you're not worth our ending up in prison. But if you move an inch, I promise you won't ever walk again.' Luke pointed his gun at his legs.

Dix kept on. 'You gonna call the cops? Mess up your schedule, lot of paperwork down at the station. And besides, your word against mine. I'm an old pal of Tori's. We look like regular businessmen, and you look like drugged-out hippies.'

Lonny was furious. 'You watch what you say, dogface. Like they'd believe you and not us!'

Luke touched his brother's arm. 'They've got a point. Long messy day with a lot of explaining. I got a better idea. Find their car keys. And all their wallets. Tori, pack up your stuff again. Lubbock, you know what to get.'

While the SUV guys glared, Luke and Lonny held them at gunpoint; the two other band boys and Tori did their job speedily.

Lubbock was out the door and back in moments with rope and duct tape.

When the SUV guys were tied up and their mouths covered, Tori took a last, backward glance at Dix. This time he was in the rocking chair, trussed up like a turkey ready for the Thanksgiving roasting pan. For the first time she understood the expression – if looks could kill. She shivered. Somehow she knew she'd be running into Dix again.

Tori and her heroes left the room. Making bets about how long it would be until the dorks would be found and what story they would come up with.

Tori wanted to know; she asked Luke. 'With those noisy gunshots, how come nobody came to investigate?'

Luke smiled, 'Around here everybody's got guns and people have a habit of minding their own business. I knew we were okay.'

Tori watched the boys letting the air out of the SUV tires.

Ready to leave, they duct-taped the 'Do not disturb' sign on the broken-locked door. And for good measure they wrapped a towel on the doorknob. Luke grinned. The almost universal sign that something sexy was happening inside – keep out. That would delay those guys being found.

As they headed for the band bus, Luke gave her a brotherly hug. 'Promise, you'll find me again when you're eighteen?'

'That's a deal. Right now, I'm thinking *huevos rancheros* for breakfast.'

'Good choice.'

Part Five
The Search

Twenty-One
Stakeout

It's a long time since we've been on a stakeout. This time we're working in daylight. We are parked across the street from the Starbucks which Izzy showed us from the back yard of his house. Excuse me, his castle, as the girls call it. So far he's robbed six Starbucks and I'm betting his 'local' will be next.

Nothing has changed. My girls are stuffed in my Chevy wagon. Evvie still gets to sit in the front with me. The other three are jammed in the back. Why jammed? Because they've brought the same items as before: a basket full of supplies; knitting needles, balls of yarn. Playing cards. Sandwiches. Snacks. Drinks. Blankets, even though it's 85 degrees outside, ditto flashlights, even though it's brightly sunny outside. All because they were on their take-to-stakeout list. Said items are on their laps and on the floors and under their feet. In the back seat, Bella sits wedged in the middle between Sophie and Ida. Alas, the *kvetching* is the same.

'Stop crowding me.' Bella.

'Stop complaining.' Ida.

'You're squishing my stomach.' Bella.

Sophie, to Ida, 'Pass me a donut. One with jelly in it.'

'You get jelly on my seat covers, you will know worse pain than in your legs.' That comes from me.

Evvie, laughing, 'I'll take a cruller.'

That's the basic routine.

They are a jolly crew because for a change they aren't staring into darkness, and they can window-shop out of my car windows while waiting for Izzy to show up. This is a street filled with tempting stores, most of which are open on Sunday.

The last stakeout was late at night and bathroom problems had loomed large. A possible car chase might also have occurred. With the probability of me having to follow the muscle car of a big macho guy who drove seventy-five miles an hour on the freeway, while I could only manage thirty-two driving through streets. Luckily, macho guy had left the bar and went home instead. A local address. But that's behind us. A successful closed case. This one looks to be just as easy. Izzy in drag. What a character. Coffee this time instead of banks. What will he think up next?

My girls are less jolly as time goes by with no sign of Izzy. With the realization that it's more difficult with bright sunlight beating down on us. The car's temperature is rising because I keep shutting the AC off and then on. The windows are open for breaths of air; mostly, we get waves of Florida's favorite brand of stifling heat.

'I need a break,' demands Sophie. 'I need to take a walk with my cane because my legs are stiffening up.'

Bella giggles. 'Don't let her fool you. She really wants to shop in The Dollar Store over there. She loves dollar stores.'

I am on to that ploy. Sophie's slogan is: 'I never met a sale I didn't love.'

Sophie huffs. 'Is that so terrible? I'll only be inches away. If Izzy shows up, which I personally think is doubtful, I can run back fast.'

'Not a good idea,' I say. 'If you see Izzy, he'll see you. And with your problem legs, running is not an option. You'll never get back into the car in time.'

Bella sighs. 'I also wouldn't mind a quick peek in The Dollar Store. They have such great bargains.'

Ida perks up. 'I say we vote,' sure it will be three to two. Away from Tori, she's reverted back to her usual grumpy, opinionated self.

Knowing her devious plan, I say, 'Don't bother. As boss of this operation, my rule is no distractions on stakeouts.' It reminds me of that great line in that all-girls' baseball movie, when Tom Hanks yells, 'There is no crying in baseball!' I'm just as firm. I can't resist. I borrow the line, showing them I mean it. 'There is no shopping on stakeouts!'

'Killjoy,' whispers Sophie, loud enough for me to hear.

Another dreary hour goes by. Dramatic complaints about sweating, and failure of deodorants. Worries that our water supply will be gone. I doubt it, since they brought eight gallons. Also that the water is getting warm. They insist they can only drink ice water. I know better.

Next up will be the necessary bathroom breaks. I tune the mumbling out. I am a cruel taskmaster. It's a matter of been there, done that, with them. Ya give 'em a hand, they take an arm.

To pass away the waiting time, Evvie and I have been taking turns reading books. I read, she watches. She reads, I watch. Now I'm reading. Another great British mystery written by Agatha Christie.

Evvie is the one on duty, and suddenly she elbows me. 'Look. Up. There.' I glance to where she's pointing. Across the vacant lot to Izzy's place. There he is in his back yard.

We've been out-ed? Yup. Our stakeout has failed.

I turn the air-conditioning on full blast. And start the engine. I announce, 'Stakeout aborted.' Which wakes up my three useless private eyes, snoring in the back seat. 'Nap time over.'

We park in front of Izzy's house and I remind them again, our cover story is – we were in the neighborhood and we decided to drop in. I want to feel him out as to why he didn't go for the steal today.

Evvie says, 'Logic check. What if he asks why would we be in this neighborhood? Off our regular beaten path?'

'Why?' I can't resist. 'Because we love dollar stores.' I smirk.

Behind me I hear angry snorts.

'Delighted that you dropped in today, being that you were in my neighborhood.' He knows that we know.

'So, you want to hear about how does my garden grow?'

We are in Izzy's back yard, next to his garage and adjoining metal shed. Our backs are to the stores we just came from. Izzy is dressed in what he is presenting to us as a gardener's outfit. Denim overalls, plaid cotton shirt, dirty boots, and straw hat. With rake in hand. And an unlit corncob pipe in his mouth. The very model of a 'gentleman farmer.' I can't wait to see him at Christmas-time in his Santa costume. I bet the minute he spotted us he put on this theatrical costume, sneaky guy. He knew we would be coming after him. But I'm on to his tricks.

'You will laugh,' he continues. 'I told you of a new hobby. This is it. I am mad about succulents. Yuccas really turn me on.' He points at his pots ready to plant. Evvie pretends avid interest. The trio is still half-asleep, sitting on a scrolled iron bench, fanning themselves because of the heat. I watch Izzy's performance with cynical admiration. He should have been an actor, that phony.

Instant-farmer Izzy points and narrates. 'Here's my aloe vera. Anytime you girls want a skin cream, I'll squeeze some out for you. Do admire the perky *Yucca baccata*. And how about my tall and spiky San Pedro cactus? There's my Barbary fig. I threw in some lavender to give me pretty flowers and a wonderful aroma. The pokeweed is definitely my favorite.'

I wonder how long it took him to memorize the names on the tags.

'The best part is how little water my babies need. Energy-saving, yes? What do you think

131

– leave them in their original clay pots or plant? I'm trying to decide.'

'That important decision must be yours,' I say, tamping down the sarcasm. I let him ramble on a bit more, and then I insist we must be off to home.

Suddenly we all jump. Bells, loud bells are clanging. Almost deafening.

'What's that?' I ask Izzy, needing to shout to be heard. The girls cover their ears.

'You can set your clocks on such a noise. Every Sunday, right at noon. The church down the street rings those bells. No sleeping past noon with that racket blasting. Makes sure everybody gets to church on time.'

Over the bells, I yell, 'Well, time to head out.'

We race, ears covered, to the front of his house to get away from the noise.

As we drive away, he waves and calls, 'Drop in anytime. *Mi casa es su casa.*'

I smile sardonically, thinking – I'll get you yet, *Señor Diablo.* The costume you'll wear then will be one with gray stripes.

Twenty-Two
At the Cop Shop

Evvie and I stare at the chart on Morrie's wall. By now, we've convinced him that Grandma Bandit is good old Grandpa Bandit, in drag this time. He's definitely the one we caught last time around, robbing every SunTrust branch. And we know for sure, this time around, he's the one hitting all the Starbucks.

Morrie points out that every robbed Starbucks is circled in red. Plus there are other red circles. Morrie explains. 'We had men at many of the Starbucks. He hits a couple of them on a Wednesday, but we guessed wrong. So we send men to another one on the next Wednesday and what does he do? He doesn't go to a Starbucks, he hits Storks Coffee Shop. Pick another pattern day and he's been to Gran Formo Café or 11th Street Annex. He's always one step ahead of us. We're beginning to be laughed at. Especially in all the coffee shops in the county. This weird old "lady" holds them up and where are we? Somewhere across town at the wrong coffee shop. The ones he's already hit are mad at us for not figuring it out.'

'There's only one Starbucks left in all of Broward County,' Morrie shows us by pointing to the one black circle on the chart.

Evvie grins. 'And we know exactly where that is – right in his own back yard. He's saving the last for best. He's playing with you.'

Morrie shrugs, 'And he's practically right in my own back yard, since this station is four blocks from where Izzy lives.'

I say, 'We tried to second-guess him, too. We were on stakeout, but he was on to us. This time I know we can nab him. And we'll walk him right down here for you to meet and greet, then you can show him to his new home in his very own comfy jail cell.'

Morrie folds his arms. 'It's a guess what day he'll choose this next time.'

I shake my head. 'He's too smart. He'll smell you a mile away, and he'll go elsewhere. We know exactly how to get him, using his own old tricks. Let us take over.'

'But what if he's armed?'

Evvie and I giggle. 'Not likely,' I say. Remember his "weapon" last time?'

Morrie laughs, too, remembering the fake gun in the deli sandwich. 'He's upped his class. This time he's using a baguette.'

Evvie can't resist. 'If he isn't at the coffee shops, he's busy gardening.'

That cracks both of us up. 'Come on, Morrie, let us be the ones laughed at if we're wrong.'

'Okay, I'll give you one shot at it. Better not embarrass me by failing.'

'Not a chance.'

'And afterwards, I want no soft-hearted "let him out on bail". I know you girls.' Morrie walks us to the door. 'How are you doing on you other "case", the mysterious Tori and Grandma Ida?'

'Slow but steady,' comments Evvie.

'Mostly slow,' I grumble. 'She's still wandering around and we haven't a clue why or what or who she's looking for. Driving Ida crazy.'

'And what about my dad?'

I smile. 'He's keeping away, leaving us to work it out.'

'By the way,' Morrie can't resist chortling, 'about

your pal, Izzy, again. Hope you guess the right day for his next heist. Maybe you should see a gypsy and get a reading.'

Even though I know he cares, my son-in-law still treats us as if we're cute, silly little old ladies. He considers us playing at being private eyes, even though he knows all our successes. I guess it's just a male thing. I adore him anyway.

With all the information on Izzy's chart in hand, we are shown out on to the street. He'll eat his words when we solve his case.

Wait till I tell Jack we are partnered with Morrie. He'll get a kick out of it.

Twenty-Three
The Retirement Home

Tori stands outside the door of this small stucco house in the area called Sunrise. She looks around making assumptions. There was an attempt at a lawn and garden that failed. A few straggly daisies tried to push their way through some grass and cement. No one named Woodley who is living here has gardening skills. A child's broken tricycle lies near the front step. The house needs painting. A home in trouble.

She thinks this means disappointment. Young child, young parents. Probably no older folks. But, anyway, she's here, and this Woodley is next on her list. She had tried calling, but kept getting the answering machine.

She rings the doorbell. Hears chimes inside. She waits. Nothing. Tries knocking. Nothing. Assumes no one is home. But she rings one more time.

The front door opens slightly. A small shape peers out at her.

'Hello. My name is Tori. May I talk to you?'

The door widens slightly. 'You're already talking to me.'

She faces a small child, maybe seven or eight. Curly reddish hair, bright blue eyes and with what looks like jam on his face. Cute little guy. Clothes on backward. Socks don't match.

'Is your mother home?'

'No.'

'Your father?'

'He doesn't live here anymore.'

Oops. Divorce? Is Woodley Mom's married or single name? How do I find out?

'Maybe Grandma?'

'She's dead.'

The child hops from leg to leg, his hand still on the doorknob.

Oops again. What does she do now? 'How about your grandfather?'

'He's at Place of Peace.'

Oh, oh, another dead relative. Then, realizing; 'Are you home all alone?'

'I have a babysitter.'

'Oh, where is she?'

'She's in the living room; she's very busy with her friends on her Facebook.'

136

This is a waste of time. 'Your last name is Woodley. Right?'

'Yup.'

'Could you tell me your mother's first name?'

'Ask her yourself. She gets home at four.' He's now jumping in place.

She's losing this kid's interest. One last try. Would this child even know? 'What's your grandparents' first names?' Has she found the right Woodley family too late?

'Grandma was Betty and you can ask Grandpa yourself.'

'How can I do that if he's at his place of peace?'

'You just go to room 311. But it's a waste of time. He won't remember you. When I go to see him he calls me Don, but that's my uncle's name.'

Aha! Not dead. A retirement home.

'Thanks, not Don. But you shouldn't open doors to strangers.'

'Okay.'

With that he slams the door in her face.

Place of Peace is in Plantation off of University Drive near West Broward. Not too far from Lanai Gardens and her not-so-beloved Grandma Ida.

Good name for it. A lot of peace and quiet. Large lawn, too well-kept, with nobody out on it. She walks up the driveway to an all-white building. Silence everywhere. Even the birds seem to keep away. Too depressing?

Tori decides not to ask anyone anything. Just walk in like she belongs there and see what happens. Since there's only one floor, she'll follow the number 3s till she finds Grandpa Woodley.

So far, so good. Inside, and no one is paying any attention to her. Nurses busily moving back and forth. Wheelchaired seniors lining the walls doing nothing, some dozing. I hope Grandpa is in his room.

There is a kind of odor everywhere. Sprayed stuff to hide old-age smells? She is not sure she ever wants to get old. Grandpa and Grandma Steiner were so disgusting; what's the point?

Here's the room. She looks in. Good. Only one bed, one person, and surely the old guy lying there watching TV must be Mr Woodley.

She knocks lightly and walks in.

'About time you got here. Did you bring the corned beef?' He grumps at her.

Guess he thinks I'm family. 'Sorry, I forgot.'

He looks puzzled. 'Or was it pastrami?'

A nurse stops at the door, and glares at her. 'How could you break the rules? You need to wear the uniform at all times! Or don't bother to come.'

A young girl of about sixteen walks past and Tori sees her dressed in a red and white outfit. And she gets it. She's a candy-striper – a high school volunteer.

'Sorry. I forgot; I'll remember next time,' Tori tells the nurse, lying easily.

The nurse huffs and walks off.

Tori smiles at the elderly man. 'Hello, Mr Woodley.'

He lifts up a book on his side table. 'Read! Read! About time you got here.'

She takes the book and pretends to look puzzled. 'But I forgot your first name.'

He grins. 'Hey, that's my routine. I remember everything damn well, but they expect me to be senile, so I don't disappoint them.'

They smile at one another. 'I promise to keep your secret.'

'Who are you? You aren't Susie, my usual candy-striper.'

'My name is Tori Steiner and I'm trying to find a Mr and Mrs Woodley who were friends with my parents, Fred and Helen Steiner. They used to live in Florida, then moved to California. I'm looking for a couple who would be in their fifties or so. A daughter or son, perhaps? Are they in that age group?'

'I'm Dick Woodley. My son, who left my daughter-in-law and his child, and whom I shall never forgive, is Stuart, and his unhappy wife is Polly. They are in their thirties and I need to disappoint; I'm sure they never knew your parents.'

Tori can't hide her frustration. 'I'm so sorry I bothered you.' Tori starts for the door.

Mr Woodley asks, 'Does that mean you won't read to me?' He winks at her.

Tori returns, smiling, and pulls a chair to sit on next to the bed. She opens the book. 'My pleasure,' she says, smiling, and starts reading.

Twenty-Four
Sophie and Bella go Shopping

Sophie waves her cane eagerly at the glistening turquoise car making its way toward them. 'Here he comes,' she says, poking Bella's arm.

'His car matches my sneakers,' Bella says happily.

They are waiting at what used to be their special getaway place, at the front gate of Lanai Gardens. Far enough away so that they won't be seen by Gladdy or Evvie or Ida. A place to wait, when they want to do something that maybe the others wouldn't approve of. Like today.

For a moment, they see no one at the wheel. Is the car driving itself? No, it's just short, funny-looking Izzy, as expected. Their driver pulls up and jumps out, with a dazzling bow from the waist practically to the cement. A car so big and a driver so little.

Bella pinches Sophie. 'Look how dressed up Izzy is?' She giggles every time she does an 'Izzy is' comment. 'He's wearing splats on his black-and-white shoes.'

'I think those are called spats. Wonder where he got those old styles.'

Bella claps her hands. They can hear music

blasting from his radio. '"Oh! My Papa"! I love that song. I hope he leaves that Eddie Fisher on.'

'Forget the music,' Sophie says, sounding like a person who would carry a whip. 'We are going out on a serious mission.'

Bella sighs. 'You always have to be a party pooper.'

Sophie pretends a great interest in cars, as if she knows anything about that subject. 'Love your wheels,' she says, wanting to sound hip. 'Is it new?'

Izzy grins. 'You are looking at a piece of history. This is a gen-u-wine Ford Edsel V-8 coupé I purchased in 1959. Color, *Light Aqua*, a beauty. People laughed when I bought it.'

He waits for a response; the girls have no idea what he expects them to say.

Izzy gives them a short auto lesson. 'It was Henry Ford's first and only failure. Named for his son. His timing was off. I paid two thousand bucks brand new and they were glad to be rid of it.'

The girls, unmoving and clueless, are waiting for a punch line.

'Guess. Guess how much it's worth today?' He snaps his fingers.

Sophie tries. 'Two thousand, five hundred?'

Izzy is peacock proud. 'Not even close, babe. It's now an antique. I've already been offered forty-one thousand!'

'Wow!' both girls say dutifully. In awe, but they don't know why, really.

With another gallant bow, their snazzily outfitted

141

chauffeur opens the door for them. 'Hop in and let's take care of those hurting legs.'

On their way to Miami Beach, Izzy asks, 'How come you didn't call for an Uber? Or Lyft? They are everywhere and cheaper than a taxi. Not that I mind driving you, as long as it isn't next Tuesday, when I'm gonna be busy.

'What's anuber?' Bella asks.

'You know. You hit the app on your iPhone . . .'

'What's an ap? And we don't got any of those phones.'

'Never mind. Forget I asked.'

Izzy pulls into the garage at what looks like a high-rise fancy hotel, within a row of many luxurious hotels along the famous beach. The girls are surprised.

Sophie wants to know, 'There's a marijuana dealer in here?'

'Trust me. Did you remember your note from your doctor?

Sophie opens her purse and waves it aloft.

'Okay, let's get you some drugs.'

The girls have had long excited discussions about what will happen today. They expect to go down some dark alley. Izzy will then knock three times on a door using a secret password. Maybe they will even meet guys with guns?

Instead, Izzy directly traverses through the gilded lobby to find the lavish gift shop in this very expensive hotel. The woman behind the counter is introduced to us as Grandma Bubba. Grandma is easily eighty-five years old, but either she is in denial, or just because she lives in Miami Beach, her hair is bleached blonde, cut short, at a stylish angle, with bangs. Her outfit is a fire-engine-red satin blouse, with a short, short matching twirly skirt. Four-inch high heels, glittery-gold strappy shoes; one could fall down on one's face in such heels. And jewelry! Necklace, dangling earrings, wristwatch. Many rings, diamonds galore; enough to weigh a lesser woman down.

She and Izzy hug so tightly, and for so long, you would think they were auditioning for parts in a senior porno flick.

Sophie whispers to Bella, 'All she's missing is rings in her nose.' Bella sniggers.

Bubba Esther looks Sophie and Bella over, writing them off – definitely low class. But if Izzy brought them, they must have money . . . okay . . .

The girls are insulted.

Izzy informs his eager buyers that Bubba's whole family lives in the penthouse. 'Bubba's son owns the hotel. This is a little sideline for his mom.'

The girls snort. Sophie whispers, 'A nice Jewish grandma; part-time saleslady and part-time drug dealer.'

Bubba Esther places an out-to-lunch sign on the gift-shop door and locks up. The girls follow Bubba and Izzy, eyes wide open, shivering in excitement. This is becoming an adventure. But excitement tamps down a bit when they enter a dreary storeroom and once again a door is locked. Much like what they'd expected earlier.

143

Bubba, with a flourish, dramatically pulls aside a thin green satin curtain. 'Voilà!'

'Who's Viola?' Bella wants to know.

'Shh,' cautions Sophie. 'Just pay attention.'

Bubba starts her pitch, standing in front of a long industrial table filled with products. 'What's your pleasure, ladies? Flowers? Concentrates? Edibles? Drinkables? Smokes?'

The girls are startled.

'Dabs, oils, hash, wax? Vapor pen. Canna tonic? Tinctures? Capsules?' She takes a breath, 'New product, strains, just in, 'Train Wreck', a sativa-dominant hybrid from California. A great help with body pains.'

Izzy sees the turned-down faces from this confusing oversell, and stops his rich saleslady friend. 'Let's keep it simple, Bub. Maybe some gummy bears and a few chocolate lollypops thrown in.'

The girls' eyes light up.

Izzy and the woman go into detailed discussion as to what's in the items; not one word is understood by the listeners. But they do manage a smile when sugar, as one of the ingredients, is mentioned. They can dig that.

Sophie tries to squeeze a word in. 'I don't want to turn into a drug addict . . .'

'Nah,' says Izzy. 'I wouldn't do that to you. They're all made from healthy phenotypes, non-psychoactive. We'll write down how much to take and you'll be all set.'

Bella tugs at Sophie. 'Maybe with an eensie-weensie bit of kick to it? Just for fun?'

Sophie hesitates, then nods. 'Very teensie-weensie.'

'Got it.' says Izzy. He picks up a package. 'This one is guaranteed "just for fun".'

The girls nod their heads, happily – yes for gummy bears.

More mumbo jumbo, then Bubba Esther hands Sophie a bill, to be paid by cash only, and immediately. Sophie gulps a few times, then forks over a price more than a month's rent.

On the way home Sophie, curious, asks Izzy, 'How do you know so much about marijuana?'

'And where did you meet that Bubba Esther?' Bella asks.

Izzy smiles. 'Ask me no questions, I'll tell you no lies.' Izzy's huge Edsel arrives at Lanai Gardens. The girls pile out. Sophie says thanks, profusely, eager to try her new 'MJ.'

Izzy says, 'Read the directions carefully. You don't want to overdose. Gummys can last as long as five hours, so watch out. And happy trails.'

Izzy drives off with a toot-toot of his horn of the great big expensive car.

The girls sneak their way back to their apartments. Bella worries. 'If someone sees us it'll be all over Lanai Gardens in five minutes. They'll wanna know where we went and what we bought. Move fast.'

Luckily, it's nap time.

145

Twenty-Five
Come Fly with Me

A gentle knock on Sophie's door. Sophie opens it quickly and practically drags Bella in. It's only seven a.m., and Bella is puzzled. One pajama-wearing woman-in-second-childhood faces the other. Sophie in her Minnie Mouse pj's; Bella in her Tweetie Pie's.

'What kind of *mishigas* is going on so early in the morning? So you need to call me?' Bella asks anxiously. 'Did you fall out of the bed again?'

Sophie wrings her hands. 'It's my legs, still killing me. I took my gummy bears and poof, nothing! Still a hundred per cent agony.'

'When did you take him and how much?'

'The directions said start with five milligrams, so I did. Ten minutes ago.'

'Let me see the directions.' Bella reaches for the pamphlet, then, 'Oops, I didn't bring my glasses. Read it to me.'

'It said wait an hour, but I can't wait, my legs are screaming, help me, help me!'

'Tell them to shush up and let's wait a little longer.'

The girls sit down at the kitchen table with the little package of multicolored cannabis gummy bears in front of them. Bella picks one up, admiringly. 'They're so cute.'

146

'Tick-tock, tick-tock, the clock moves so slowly.' Sophie gets up and fills the kettle.

'Don't complain. Every tick and every tock makes us older.'

'You're right. What kind of tea? Want your usual?'

Bella shakes her head. 'No Lucky Dragon today, maybe Coconut Crush?'

'I'm drinking Herbal Delight. Do you think that goes good with gummys?' Sophie looks up at the kitchen clock and sighs. Only fifteen minutes later.

Bella says slyly, 'Could I try one, just for fun?'

'Sure, why not? They're useless. I might ask for my money back.'

Bella takes her time picking out a color she likes. Pink is always a favorite. She's torn between the pink and purple, her other favorite color. Pink wins. She tastes it on her tongue, then swallows. 'Sweet as sugar,' she says, approvingly. Now Bella also looks at the clock.

Sophie pours the tea. Then, suddenly, 'I can't stand it. I'm taking a second dose. Maybe it'll work faster. So far these drugs are overrated.' She pops another gummy.

'What the heck, I'll join you. Purple this time. It's like eating candy. Ha-ha, it is candy, sort of.'

Sitting, moping, drinking tea, and waiting, feet tapping the minutes away. Sophie tosses out another 'Tick-tock.' She pulls at the neck of her pj's. It's getting hot in here. 'I'm turning on the air.' Jumping up out of her chair, and forgetting her cane, she hops and skips into the living room where her wall switch lives. 'Hot. Hot. Hot,' she says, turning the dial. Then she rushes to her windows and opens them all, as well, which she knows will undermine the AC, but she doesn't care.

Bella is right behind her. 'Guess what? I'm hungry.'

'So, eat. Who's stopping you?'

Bella goes back into the kitchen, opens the freezer and takes out a frozen bagel. 'I'm gonna eat this.'

'What's the "this"?' Sophie trots back into the kitchen.

Bella is standing next to Sophie's small yellow radio, with its colorful Minnie Mouse sticker. 'I'm microwaving.' She keeps poking the bagel onto the top of the radio.

'I'm hungry, too,' says puzzled Sophie. 'Where do you keep the Fritos?'

'I don't know. Who lives here?' Bella says, looking around, and under the kitchen table, as if searching for clues.

The radio suddenly blasts on. Latin music. Loud! Bella jumps away. She's amazed and delighted. 'I never heard of a microwave that plays songs.' She continues poking the bagel onto the top, still with no luck.

Sophie jabs Bella in her belly. 'I do. I do.'

'What do you "do, do"?'

'I don't know. Fritos, Fritos where are you?' She opens and closes one cabinet door after another.

'I am not fat!' Bella is furious.

'Who said you were?'

'Were what?'

'I never met a Frito I didn't like.' Sophie now

148

tosses bags of chips from her shelves onto the floor.

Bella leans her ear close to the radio. 'Bagel, bagel, get warm, already.'

'I feel like dancing.' The radio plays a medley of soft Cuban love songs. Sophie cups her ear to listen, then asks, 'Salsa, good for you?'

'Salsa is good.'

Sophie kicks off her bunny slippers and begins to dance. Bella plays follow-the-leader. Soon they are dancing together to the imagined salsa rhythm. Then back to back. Then twisting each other around. Sophie goes to the radio and turns the sound way up. An announcer now does an anti-diarrheal commercial. In Spanish.

Sophie is back to her dancing partner. 'What are we dancing?' Bella wants to know.

'Feels like a cha-cha to me,' Sophie says through chomping on chips. She dances them out of the kitchen and back into the living room. Bella still grips her frozen bagel.

'I didn't know you cha-cha'd.'

Sophie whirls her arms and fists this way and that, looking more like a boxer than a dancer. 'Maybe it's a rumba. Who knows? Who cares.' She pushes the sofa out of her way for extra dancing space.

The radio now is tuned to the news of the day. In Spanish.

Whirling dervishes, they are. Happy, happy, making up steps. Louder, louder. Faster, faster.

What's that, someone is knocking on my wall?

A shout comes from the adjoining balcony, 'Keep it down, idiot!'

149

Sophie picks up her cane and uses it to knock back on her side of the same wall. 'Shtupid Shhelma, next door. Shhe complains about everyshing.' Sophie's blurry tongue yells louder. 'Shhhut up!'

Sophie leans Bella down into a dip. The dancing continues.

Twenty-Six
Back to the Pool

We're on our way to the pool again. It was closed for a few days to empty it of all dregs of the dreaded alligator. Scrubbed down and ready for use again, though our neighbors return for their morning swim with trepidation and terrifying memories of the ugly lizard. Frankly, I think it was more afraid of us than we of it. Jack suggests the Thing didn't like the chlorine. Joe and Evvie are of the opinion it was a 'she', and she was lost and was resting on her way back to Alligator Alley, the bizarrely named two-lane tollway connecting the east to west, aka Interstate 75. Fort Lauderdale to Naples. A steamy path through the Everglades where alligators and worse cross the road. Ugh, we've been on it. It? Him? She? Whatever.

Eyes dart toward the wooded area, fearful of another cold-blooded, scaled reptile showing up. Gone was our alligator, taken who-knows-where by those amazing wranglers. Bella, always with the perfect non sequitur, swears she'll never buy alligator shoes or purses again. It would be too much like killing a relative she hates.

The girls are in a good mood. Bella suggests, 'I guess we might go in the pool. Or not. I don't want to run into my relatives again.'

We all laugh and look to Ida. Ms Snippy doesn't snap at Bella. She's still not back to her old self. Her eyes are on Tori, walking ahead of us.

Surprise. Tori, who has not been seen for a while, has deigned to give us the honor of her surly presence. She doesn't look too happy. She's downright grouchy. Whatever she's looking for – and I assume she is on some quest – has not been found. And why she is staying with Ida remains a puzzle, since the bad feelings are still rampant. Poor Ida continues to take any meanness the girl dishes out.

Uh-oh, there's Hy on full throttle holding forth. Hy, wearing his usual garish Hawaiian shorts, is standing and addressing everyone around the pool. Even the snowbirds at their far end, what we have nicknamed South of Canada, are paying attention.

Hy is telling his tasteless jokes. Oh, oh, once again, he's stealing from the famous comics like Joey Adams, Milton Berle, Jackie Mason. Hy is an equal opportunity thief: he'll steal from anyone. Everyone's laughing, even though they've heard them all before.

'I just came back from a pleasure trip. I dropped my mother-in-law off at the airport. Va voom! What are three words a woman making love doesn't want to hear? Honey, I'm home. Va voom! We stayed at a hotel with a water bed. My wife called it The Dead Sea.'

Hy stops at the sight of Tori. This could spell disaster. The misogynist and the sarcastic girl could shoot off fireworks.

We go to our usual lounge chairs. I explain to Tori that by now these chaises are marked in blood. Everyone has had his or her place on the grass rim around the pool for years and change is unacceptable. You do not ever, ever take your pool stuff into a territory not your own. She ignores my lecture; old ladies are a bore.

Ida tenses; this is now her default demeanor. She slinks down into her chaise next to Jack and me. Evvie and Joe take their regular seats on the other side of us. Sophie and Bella are chuckling in anticipation of trouble, and Sophie is sitting in a chair instead of lying down, in hopes of being able to get up again. I wonder what's up with those two. They are non-stop gigglers these days.

Tessie and Sol are bobbing up and down in the shallow end of the pool like two demented water buffaloes at play. Tessie bobs but Sol, much shorter, gargles up pool water.

Across the way, Hy and Lola are already settled in. Lola is knitting another one of her many long, long scarves. By now the length would be down to her knees. Since there is never a scarf day in steamy Florida, I wonder what she does with them. Maybe it's like that new coloring book craze. Older people coloring in kiddy books, and remember not to let your crayon go over a line. You do it, just to do it. It's supposed to keep you calm.

Jack pulls an empty chair near us for Tori. She drops her towel and tee shirt on it; she is wearing her same revealing bikini. Her eyes are on Hy, his are on her; such staring, they're both looking like they just ate ice cream and are licking their lips, orbs huge as searchlights at an opening night on Broadway.

All of us shudder and hold our breath. It's like watching a mongoose size up the snake. Or is it the snake sizing up the mongoose?

Hy emotes with his hands. Waving them, shaking them. Wiggling them. His body dances up and down, his butt wobbling, too. Now, directed at Tori, to impress.

'I tell ya. What a day. I *owned* Hialeah yesterday afternoon. I could do no wrong. All I had to do is bet on anything that came out of Panorama Stables. First, I caught the double with Temple Star and Glory Girl. Boy, did they pay off. Then another wild ride in the third race with an exacta. The fifth won me a long shot, Miss M and M, a nag wearing blinders. Win. Win. Win. Everybody! Drinks are on the house!' Which he knows is ridiculous, since we all bring our own plastic water and juice bottles and booze is not allowed.

Hy is surprised at the sound of applause.

And there's Tori clapping with gusto. 'Bravo!' Hy looks her up and then down. Delighted it's coming from the gorgeous young thing, the one staying with Ida. 'Well, hel-lo, hot stuff!' He gives a shrieking wolf whistle and we all wait for hell to break loose.

'Well, hel-lo, back to you.' A simpering voice. Simpering?

He pats his chaise lounge, indicating an invitation to sit at his side. 'Just sashay your luscious self on over here.'

And Tori indeed 'sashays'. We are in shock. Tori, ice maiden? Tori is not slicing and dicing him with sarcasm? She's invited into enemy territory? Lola is sending eye daggers. She's the only one in the world who thinks Hy is hot stuff and she wants no competition from this teenybopper.

Hy straightens out his beach towel that reads, 'Stolen from the Miami Hilton', and Tori sits daintily down.

He pours them two glasses of iced tea. They don't notice the ice emanating from Lola, knitting furiously.

'Funny you should mention that Panorama Horse group; I grew up in a town called Panorama City,' Tori says.

'Nice name,' he responds.

'Shoulda been called Puke City. Crummy place. Every kid had a knife in his pocket.'

'Sounds as awful as my hometown. On the lower west side of New York. Right next to the old Meat Packing district. The smells of dead animals could asphyxiate you. Or make you upchuck.'

'We were so poor, cat food was considered a luxury.'

'We were so poor, my dad made me crawl in the gutters digging for pennies.'

By now the avid outdoor pool theater-goers

154

are punching each other in amazement. This is great TV. Remember the old *Can You Top This?*

Our group is stunned to see that Tori has suddenly become a motor-mouth. And we have never, in all these years, heard any of his background from Hy. Everyone, including those actually in the pool, is leaning in, breathless, not wanting to miss a beat.

Now Hy is rubbing sunblock cream over her back and Tori is making mewling noises of pleasure. I hope that Lola won't do her own leaning in and kill her with one of her knitting needles.

They are still at it. Taking turns. I'll do your back, you do mine. Oh boy, trouble, right here in River City. Where are the trombones?

Hy says, 'When I was born, my father took one look at me and ran away from home. He said he was only going out for cigarettes. For a long time we lived in our old Ford V8.'

'I was born in a jail cell with a bunch of cons watching.'

'My mom couldn't hold down a job, so she just sat in the car and drank anything she could get her hands on.'

'Hah! That's nothing. My mother and father robbed banks. When they were escaping from the cops, they ended up in a storm drain. My father drowned and my mother was caught. So I get to share my birth date with my father's death.'

I gasp. I can't believe she's revealing to Hy all the things she refused to tell us. And what about Hy? Telling her astonishing things we've never heard from him before.

155

'Get this one.' Hy, still at it, 'I had to dress myself in the car, pee in the bushes, then go off to school without breakfast.'

'I had to live with my grandparents from hell, because my other grandma abandoned us.' Tori raises her finger and points at Ida. 'And there she is.'

I can see Ida next to me, thoroughly miserable.

'Hey, kid, so why are you here?' Hy asks, the man known around here as Mr Subtlety. Asking the question that was on all of our minds. Now we'll find out.

Tori is just about to answer him when Ida jumps up and screams at her. 'Stop it! Stop it! I can't take any more.'

Tori halts all information, clams up, and we lose our chance to finally know!

The girls and I hide our disappointment.

Lola growls at Hy. He's in big trouble now. I'd love to be a fly on their wall tonight.

Ida races away from the pool.

The Canadians are gossiping like mad.

The show is over. Swim time is ended.

Part Six
The Follow-Up

Twenty-Seven
Happy Anniversary

The champagne is flowing; the soft-shell-crab appetizer happily being chewed. Evvie and Joe, Jack and yours truly are celebrating our double one-year wedding anniversary. The restaurant is one of these new, have-to-go-to boutique places. Important chef, unique and delicious food, tiny portions, high prices. But what the hey – we've snuck away from Lanai Gardens to celebrate privately. This evening, our many friends there are throwing a party for us, but this lunchtime event, we're on our own.

We are seated at an outdoor patio on spindly, uncomfortable wrought-iron seats and at a much-too-petite café table, but we don't care. Everything else is perfect. We have each other; we have our health, and enough dough for a once-a-year expensive meal splash.

The weather is ideal. Gussied up in fancy dress-up cocktail-hour clothes for the occasion. No shorts and tee shirts this afternoon.

We reminisce about our dual wedding, which ended up with a wild chase after a psychotic killer.

'There you were, waiting under the *chuppah* for your bride to stroll down the aisle, and your French tootsie traipsed down instead . . .' says I.

159

'Grrr, she was not my French tootsie,' Jack says, giving my cheek a pretend pinch.

Evvie laughs. 'Well, she wanted to be your French tootsie.'

'Beside the point! Your bride-to-be was almost killed.' I jump in again.

Joe adds to it. 'What a sight, everyone at the wedding party leaping on top of that crazy guy, beating him with their canes! Not a foot soldier under seventy-five!'

'And the rabbi didn't know whether he should marry me to the wrong woman.' Jack smirks.

We are rolling with laughter about those mad moments; and suddenly Jack pokes me lightly, his voice turns serious. 'Look, there, down at the corner. Everyone look! Quickly!'

All eyes turn and peer. Evvie wants to know what we're looking at.

Jack points, 'Isn't that our Tori getting into a cab?'

'I see her,' I say. 'It is definitely Tori.'

By now, she's climbed inside, and I can see her bending over to speak to the driver. I jump up. 'Quick, let's go!'

We all leap out of our chairs. Jack throws down a fistful of money on the table. Joe adds to it and we dash for our car, which, luckily, is only steps away.

'Don't lose them, honey!' I tell my husband. Jack drives, positioning himself three cars behind the back of the cab.

Joe, leaning over the back seat, is baffled. 'Why are we doing this? We didn't even have our main course.'

I answer. 'Tori has been teasing all of us with

160

her strange behavior toward Ida, ever since she arrived. We know she disappears every day, so we are now going to find out where she goes and what she's up to.'

Joe wonders, 'Will the restaurant hold our lunch for us? I was really looking forward to the lobster thermidor.'

Evvie reminds him. 'That *tiny* portion of lobster.' She kisses him gently on his cheek. 'You always wanted to know what our PI biz is like. Now you get to watch it in action. We chase clues when we can get them. And today, we might find out something about the elusive Ms Tori.'

'Oh, all right, but couldn't we have followed her on a day when we weren't having lobster?'

'Good point,' Evvie agrees, smiling at him. 'But, no.'

'Got to follow when opportunity knocks.' Jack, even though retired, still has that bloodhound quality of a good cop, sniffing at a good lead. He sharply turns left when the cab does. Then right again. Little by little the neighborhood is changing, from middle class to a street that has seen better times. The cab stops abruptly.

'Catch the house number, hon,' Jack says. 'I'm going to drive past.'

'Hon' is right on the job, and the address is duly noted.

When we go around the corner and come back again, we see the cab is still waiting and Tori is talking to a woman who has answered the door.

Jack informs us, 'We've got to keep going, suss out what you can.'

161

I relate, 'Woman is in her forties, wearing an apron, probably interfered with *her* lunch.' I make a guess. 'Seems like Tori doesn't know her, nor does the woman know Tori.'

Evvie adds, 'She probably told the cabbie to wait, so this a quick stop. Looking for someone or trying to get info.'

Jack drives around the block and back to the same street once again. This time he pulls into a space close by from where we can watch Tori. We wait until Tori says goodbye, the woman goes back inside and the cab drives away.

'Ready?' I say to Jack.

'Hold on,' my hubby says, with a straight face. 'I'm not a registered member of Gladdy's Girls.' He folds his arms across his chest. 'I'll just stay here with Joe. Let you super-gals do your thing.'

Evvie and I exchange glances. She nods.

I say, 'Well, I've just appointed you a member – at least for today. You're the right one for the job.'

Jack teases, 'I don't know.' He pauses, dragging it out. 'You always say no to mixing business with pleasure.'

Oops, he's throwing my words back at me. 'Sometimes business goes along with pleasure.'

Jack winks. 'I'm happy with my job as boy-toy.'

I hit him playfully on his shoulder. He pretends to pull away in pain.

We all have a good laugh at that.

'Ready?' I say to him, brigadier general to lowly private.

Evvie knows what we're going to do, and explains to her baffled Joe that we hope to find

162

out what information Tori wanted from the woman.

Joe has his hand on the door handle, about to get out.

Jack, now on board, explains to Joe, 'We can't all go, that would make the woman suspicious.'

Evvie agrees. 'Joe and I will stay here. You'll do better, Jack, with your police ID card.'

'Hey, we're talking *expired* police ID card. It's against the law for me to use it. You wanna get me arrested?' He grins.

Evvie makes a pretext of looking both ways. 'Don't see any cops around here, do you?'

Jack answers with an eyebrow raise. 'Some sister-in-law. You want me to break the law?' Joe and I also pretend to look for the law to pounce on my dear, honest husband. We look both ways. 'All clear,' Joe says, getting with it.

Jack argues. 'Besides, I was a cop in New York, never in Florida . . .'

'What if it doesn't work?' worries Joe.

I answer. 'If all else fails, we can always tell the truth.'

'Oh. Okay.' Then sly, 'We go back to our lunch, after?' Joe is tenacious about his meals. We ignore him.

It's been decided. Today he is Jack, the scofflaw. Game plan – husband and I will go play good-cop-bad-cop, or no cop at all. Whatever it takes. Our co-conspirators will remain in the car.

Joe indicates his gurgling stomach to Evvie. 'Still hungry . . .' he sing-songs.

She gives him a quick hug. 'We can always snuggle,' Evvie promises.

163

Joe, pathetic now. 'Aw shucks. I can still smell it. That mouth-watering, reeking of garlic . . .'

'Shut up and kiss me.'

We stroll up to the door, our faces a mask of business demeanor. I ask Jack, 'Two questions. How do we not scare her off if she smells trouble? And how do we explain that, for cops, we're so over-dressed?'

'The first, just follow what I do. As for us being so gorgeously put together, I'll tell her we come from a precinct full of rich people.'

I laugh, then put on my game face.

The same woman opens the door and, of course, notices how dressy we are.

Jack flashes his lapsed identity card quickly, and introduces himself as the detective he once was. He passes me off as his assistant.

She informs us she's Mrs Marie Bonner. She's curious. 'Do you cops always dress this nicely?'

Jack can't resist. 'We're on our way to a stakeout at the Ritz Carlton in Miami Beach, but we needed to make this one stop.'

I hide my amusement. He could charm an alligator out of its skin.

'The girl, Gloria Steiner, just spoke to you.'

Mrs Bonner nervously comments, 'She said her name was Tori.'

I pop up, inventing as I go. 'That's her code name. We need to know why she came to see you.'

The woman frowns. 'Is she a criminal? Maybe I shouldn't have talked to her. Maybe I shouldn't talk to you.' She is worried about getting the girl in trouble.

164

Smoothy Jack gives her an endearing smile, one that could calm the same alligator out for a kill. 'No problem. She's in a teenage high-school program trying out for the police academy and we're her mentors, testing how well she did.'

Jack, quick thinker that he is, continues on, inventing a story – Tori, police trainee. The woman should only know what a pain Tori, the trainee, is.

The woman relaxes. 'The girl was very polite. You should certainly give her good marks.'

'So far, so good,' I comment, getting with the program. 'What exactly did she say to you?'

The woman folds her arms and leans on her doorjamb, totally willing to help the young student. 'She said she was looking for a couple named Woodley who lived in my house about fifteen years ago. Maybe they moved in as long ago as thirty years or so. She said it was very important to find them again. Something to do with an old unsolved crime.'

She hesitates, so I fly in again. 'Very good work on her part; that was her assignment.'

Mrs Bonner continues. 'I said she was in luck because we bought our home from the original owners. Did she mean Harvey and Lila Woodley? That was many years ago. And she said, yes, the very people she was looking for.

'Well done,' I say. 'And do you have a forwarding address for the Woodleys?'

Mrs Bonner shakes her head. 'Sorry, I don't. Then the girl thanked me and left.' Mrs Bonner

165

glances at us, looking eager. 'How did young Tori do?'

'One hundred percent,' I assured her.

We are just about to leave when she adds, 'By the way, she did say something odd. Would you like to know what?'

I shoot her a big smile. 'Every little bit helps her score.'

'She said, at least I think that's what it was; she said Hah Hah and Lie Lie and then laughed out loud. Whatever does that mean?'

'Sorry, we can't tell you. Privileged information,' I add.

The woman nods her head, accepting this most private non-answer.

So we all three shake hands and Mrs Marie Bonner, citizen do-gooder, I suppose returned happily back to her lunch. Meanwhile off we marched, looking very professional, on our way to our car.

I whisper in my darling's ear, 'How did you become such a proficient liar?'

'Practice, dearest, practice. And you were not so bad yourself.'

I muse. 'Hah Hah, Lie Lie. It's a clue, but what on earth does it mean? I have to think about it and solve the puzzle. Tori, you little devil, you.

Twenty-Eight
Reporting to Ida

I am in Ida's apartment soon after we return from our lunchtime adventure. I interrupt her frenzied vacuuming to catch her up. Housework is something she does to help her deal with her frustration with Tori. First I determine where the problematic houseguest is, in order that we not be interrupted.

'Can you believe it? She's with Hy, her new best friend.' Ida says sarcastically, as she points to the rear-view window and I look out. Sure enough, Tori and Hy are seated on a bench below, seemingly in lively conversation.

'Amazing,' I say.

'Ever since that day at the pool, they've been thick as thieves.'

'I'll talk fast in case their conversation ends, and she comes running upstairs.'

Ida can't get over our following Tori, and our chat with the housewife. 'Trying to find the Woodleys? Ida once knew them. But that was maybe thirty years ago! How odd. Why would she be looking for them? How did she even know about them?'

It gives her the courage suddenly, while Tori is still downstairs, to search for the photo in her granddaughter's backpack. 'I've got a hunch. Watch out the window and yell if she moves.'

I play at guard dog as she rifles Tori's backpack in her guest bedroom.

She holds it aloft. There is the photo she hadn't clearly seen yet. Stops to put on her glasses. 'Oh, my goodness, it's my daughter, Helen, on her wedding day to Fred, with Harvey and Lila Woodley, their closest friends. They were best man and maid of honor.'

'Now that's quite fascinating.' She hands me the photo and I turn it over.

Ida says, 'That's just scribbling. I couldn't read it.'

However, I can. 'Ida, it says The Woodleys, Ft. Lauderdale.'

'Oh, my God. I didn't realize.' Ida shoves the photo back where it belongs.

We hurriedly return to the living room and sit down on the couch, drinking tea she made when I arrived, even though now it's cold. But never mind, we are meant to be found chatting in innocent mode.

We can infer that Tori has a reason to search for these two people, but Ida can't imagine why. 'They were Florida friends, but when the family moved to California, they lost track of them. Who knows if the Woodleys are still around in Fort Lauderdale, or are even alive.'

I feel her out. 'About time to confront Tori and ask her what she's up to? Now that we know about the Woodleys.' I don't know if Tori is ready. Is Ida?

168

She sounds unsure. 'Maybe not here. Maybe if we take her out somewhere and get her alone.'

The door opens and Tori bounces in. A smile on her face.

'We were just talking about you,' I say.

Ida gulps. Turns pale.

'Yeah? What about?' Tori asks with no interest whatsoever.

I am getting used to thinking fast on my feet these days. 'I'm kind of curious. What were you and Hy gabbing about?' That's all I could come up with. I doubt she will answer.

She brightens at this. 'He's teaching me how to handicap horses. I love the racetrack language. So colorful. Trifecta, allowance, paramutual, claiming, break, maiden, payouts. It goes on and on. A whole new world.'

Nice to see the seemingly cheerful child underneath the anger. 'I remember some of those terms,' I say. 'My dad would have plunked a cot down and slept at Hialeah, if they'd let him. He loved the track.'

'Hy is going to take me out there one of these days.'

'You'll love it,' I encourage. 'However, you might consider shopping for an outfit for yourself.'

Ida releases her breath finally.

'No thanks,' says Tori.

I expect that. 'Well, you ought to know, they don't allow jeans, tee shirts, shorts or flip-flops at the racetrack. They've a pretty strict dress code.' I don't mention that these rules only apply to the fancy upper-level Turf Club. Sneaky me.

169

Lucky she's in a good mood after her talk with Hy. She looks down at herself in her typical denims and tank tops. 'Okay, we shop.'

'Great, let's all go to Sawgrass Mall on Friday,' I say, nailing it down.

'Whatever.'

Ida's color comes back in her cheeks.

Tori reaches into her pocket and pulls out a folder. 'He gave me one of his old racetrack programs. They list every horse in every race and what the odds are. I'm going to study them and learn every other phrase.'

Time out from searching for the Woodleys? I get up and start for the door so I can leave before she changes her mind.

'We can even have lunch together,' Ida manages to say, trying for brightly.

But the minute her grandmother speaks, the light goes off and Tori returns to sullen girl again. She shoves the program back into her pocket and heads for her bedroom.

I open the front door and say to Ida in a whisper, 'Make sure she sticks to our Friday date to go shopping.'

On my way downstairs, it's my turn to laugh. I've figured it out. Hah Hah – Harvey, and Lie Lie – Lila. Harvey and Lila Woodley. Gothcha, Secret Agent Tori.

Twenty-Nine
Tuesday with Izzy

The girls finally have it their way. We are stationed in their favorite dollar store across from the vacant lot below Izzy's house, next door to the last un-hit Starbucks. Sophie and Bella are ecstatically busy shopping, while Evvie and Ida are with me at the front of the store thanks to the cooperation of the manager. We are watching his every move with our binoculars. It is Tuesday, one p.m. We didn't use a gypsy, but we went through Morrie's list of dates and hit times and Tuesday jumped out at us.

Sophie and Bella seem overly giggly today. They are actually tossing things into their basket, sing-songing, 'Dollar this, dollar that . . .' Odd. I suppose it's the excitement of the hunt.

Evvie nudges me. Our boy is on the move. Sure enough, there's Izzy, with a face plied with makeup, dressed in women's clothes, wearing a woman's long-hair wig and carrying a shopping bag with a Moishe's Deli logo. He (she) daintily tiptoes his (her) way down past his house, continuing through the empty back lot heading in our direction.

'Places everybody!' I push Sophie and Bella, reluctant to leave their filled shopping carts, and shove them to the door. Everyone rushes out to their appointed positions. Inside and out of Starbucks, surrounding the store. Ida is now a 'customer,' with a big floppy hat and large glasses, who enters and sits down at a front table 'reading' a newspaper. There are a few other customers, noses down in computers, and the manager is hiding as I requested.

As soon as Izzy enters, Sophie covers the rear entrance, Bella skips to her spot in the front. Evvie is already at her hiding place.

Through the store window I see Izzy head for the cash register. I wait across the street. No hurry. We know his MO, the same *modus operandi* he's used before. It will be Evvie, ready and waiting, who makes the catch.

I wait and watch him doing his old robber shtick – 'Stick-'em-up or else' with his fake gun, this time whipped out from the inside of a baguette hidden in a tote bag from Madame Mimi's French patisserie.

I had directed the two-person staff how to play their parts. I told them to stay calm and not show any emotion at all. I sigh. Everybody wants to get into showbiz. The guy barista is pretending 'terror.' The girl barista is near 'fainting.' They practically quake as they hand the odd-looking female all the cash in the register. They are told to get down on the floor and close their eyes. Go down quietly, I had rehearsed. What the wannabee 'cast members' do instead, is swoon. All right already, enough! I had said play it with subtlety, what I got is Charlie Chaplin and Edna Purviance in the silents. All they're missing is the villain with the twirly black mustache.

172

Izzy has the money. He walks past the nerds at their computers, who heard and saw nothing with their ear buds and iPhones.

Time for me to make my entrance.

And now he's in the Ladies' Room, quickly changing back to being a male, wiping off the makeup, stuffing the loose dress and wig in the huge shopping bag, along with the dough.

To his shock, here comes Evvie, popping out of a stall, stopping him as he's about to escape out the door. Now my entrance. I come in from the front door and further block him.

'Hi, there,' is my snappy rejoinder.

'Planting some cactus in here?' Evvie says at her snarkiest.

Ida, holding the floppy hat, comes in and joins us. 'New hobby, Iz?'

Sophie and Bella, still sniggering, won't be left out, and we have a full bathroom contingency. Plus a very confused millennial girl who just walked in to use the facility and who immediately turns around and rushes out, not wanting to get involved in whatever crazy is going down.

Bella needs to ask, noting what's left of his face makeup. 'Is he Izzy?'

Sophie says, 'Yes, he is Izzy.' She laughs yet again at their little inside joke.

Our captured criminal grins at us, hands held high in capture stance. With admiration, 'You girls are good.'

And Ida has to get the last word in. 'You're a bad boy, Isadore Dix. You are under citizen arrest.'

We five march our perp out of the bathroom to applause from the actor-baristas. I calm the nervous manager down, saying the money must be held as proof, but will be returned soon. The nerds still don't look up.

We trot our way down West Broward Boulevard, looking like a happy group of city hikers. One cheerful guy, surrounded by five beaming women.

Izzy shrugs. 'Nice of me to live walking distance from the police station.'

We agree. Morrie already agreed.

Izzy's walk of shame ends at number 1300, where Morrie waits for us outside his precinct front door. No guns necessary. A clean arrest.

Morrie reads him his rights, then congratulates us. 'Good job, ladies.'

As our friend, the cop walks the relaxed and smiling crook inside, Izzy gives us last-minute instructions. 'Call up Jerry Pinsky in Plantation and tell him I'm sorry, but his hernia surgery has to wait. Also my house key is hidden under a fake rock next to the front door. Don't forget to feed my goldfish. And water the cactus.' He winks at Bella and Sophie.

The two of them nod enthusiastically. 'We will, we will,' they promise. Giggle. Giggle.

Sophie pirouettes. 'Wishhh we shoulda had this stufff fifty years . . . go.'

'At leasht,' Bella agrees.

I shake my head. If I didn't know better, I would think those two women are on drugs. Another look at them. Is it possible?

Thirty
The Goldfish Caper

Happy. Happier. Happiest. 'Whee,' shouts Sophie, 'maybe it's the Cucarasha-cha!' The girls are prancing around Sophie's apartment again. Ignoring, as usual, the pounding on the wall from her furious neighbor, Selma.

Bella twirls, then puffs for breath, linking her arms with Sophie, then asks, 'Aren't we supposed ta go ta Izzy's today to feed the goldfishhhies?' Her turn to slur.

'Shure, we wouldn't want the little darlings to pershh, no perishhh . . .'

Sophie dances Bella back into the kitchen and lifts up the gummies package, shakes it as if it was a castanet. 'One for the road?' she says, winking.

'Stop running,' Bella cries out as Sophie gallops down Oakland Park Boulevard, dangerously waving her cane about and ignoring lights and stop signs. It's a miracle traffic is slow. A bigger miracle, Sophie isn't falling down. Or getting run over. Or hit by a bus. Speaking of buses: 'We gotta catch the 81 bus and there it is!'

'Yeah, but we need to catch it in one piece,' Bella calls out worriedly. 'What about your hurting legs?'

Sophie laughs. 'My gummys are finally working. I'm feeling no pain.' She reaches the bus door, and puts one leg up on the first step. 'Look at me, lifting a leg that doesn't shriek. I'll hold the driver. Hurry, get on up!'

'I'm hurrying. I'm also dying, I can't breathe.'

Bystanders might look surprised at the two elderly ladies, running, hopping, giggling, chortling and zigzagging their way down the street, with an occasional shout of 'whoopee!'

'Quick, look on the top of the bus window, does it say eleven east?' she yells down to the puffing Bella.

'Either I get on or read numbers. I'm good for only one choice.'

'Get on!'

She hops on, muttering, 'I still think we shoulda took a taxi.'

'How many times do I have to say we can't afford it. Too 'spensive.'

Panting, they practically crawl up the steps and lean over the bus driver, sweating in his ear. Sophie, breathing hard, asks the driver sweetly. 'This is the east?'

'Yup.'

'You *will* let us off at Twelfth Avenue?' She hiccups.

The driver, ordinarily a large, jovial sort, now looks at them, askance. Passengers glance up as well. Then quickly look down again, suddenly busy with magazines, knitting, praying, whatever will avert their eyes.

Why? Because what they see is one woman (Bella), with curlers still in her hair, wearing floppy beach sandals with different-colored socks and her blouse is on backwards. The other one's (Sophie's) makeup is smeared on only half of her face, making her look like some clown. Her hair is one big frizz. The bus passengers silent verdict is: decidedly spaced-out bag ladies.

The girls flop from side to side, on their way up the aisle as the bus lurches ahead. Bella whispers to Sophie, 'We didn't pay.'

At least Bella thinks she's whispering. More like loud enough to wake the dead, so to speak.

The driver calls out, 'Never mind, ladies. It's on the house.' He knows the best way to deal with nutcases is to stay calm and play along. Until they get off.

'Good thing Glad and Ida are shopping today with Tori, so they won't notice we're gone,' says Bella.

'Too bad it was Tuesday last week, and we had to arrest Izzy. He coulda driven us today. He's such a good driver.' Sophie sighs, leaning back, stretching out, legs splayed in the aisle.

Bella sighs. 'If he wasn't in jail, he could feed his own goldfishies.' Another sigh. 'I hope they gave him a nice cell.'

Bella, at the window seat, draws lines and a circle in the dirty glass. Sophie reaches over her. Draws an X to her circles. They play tic-tac-toe.

A little while later, the ex-jovial bus driver dutifully calls out 'Twelfth Avenue.' But, by then, the girls are snoring, coming down from their drug, leaning on one another's shoulders. The driver shrugs.

177

At the end of the line, the driver shakes them awake. And practically pushes them out the door.

The gummies have sort of worn off. Now they are only mildly stoned. Sophie and Bella look around, confused. This is definitely not Twelfth Avenue. Way beyond.

Bella moans. 'We missed our stop. What do we do now?'

Sophie grabs her by the hand and pulls her. 'We cross the street and go west.'

Twenty minutes later, 81 west pulls up. Same driver. All three moan as he waves them to the back.

'Let us off at Twelfth?'

'Yeah, yeah, it will be my pleasure,' he says, no longer jovial, 'and this time stay awake.'

'The key is under the rock, just like Izzy said.' Sophie holds the key on high.

'Think Goldfishy will be glad to see us?'

'Starving and thrilled.' Sophie opens the door, then puts the key back under the rock, as previously instructed.

Bella pats her on the back in recognition of job well done. 'You remembered.'

Izzy's mansion is stuffy, but they dare not open any windows.

Bella is excited. 'You feed the fishies and water the plants; I'm itching to see the upstairs again.'

'Okay, but don't take too long. Izzy might not like us snooping. It isn't polite.'

Bella hippity-hops up the staircase. As far as she's concerned, snooping is her middle name. Sure, Izzy gave them the tour, but she wants another look-see.

She loves the old-fashioned bedrooms. All that fancy, heavy dark furniture. And that silk and satin, so neat to touch. Ooh, would she love a sleepover in this fancy place. All this luxury makes her want to sing. So, she does. She does her version of a song from Fiddler on the Roof, '*If I was a rich girl . . .*'

What's that? Is it raining? She hears the sound of running water. She parts a heavy brocaded drape and looks out the window. Sunny, just like before. The rain noise stops. She must have imagined it.

Curious, anyway, she heads in the direction of the rain sound, which takes her to a huge bathroom down around a corner. Maybe there's a leak. As she enters, she realizes it is steamy in there, the room almost all fogged in, and she can hardly see. She's on tippie-toes, now singing, 'Tiptoe Through the Tulips.' And to her amazement, an apparition appears before her eyes.

Bella gasps.

A figure, soaking wet, draped in white cotton, stands in front of a closed shower curtain, a mist encircling him.

'Oooh,' says Bella enthralled, and scared at the same time.

The figure doesn't move.

'You're a ghost. Right?' She hopes.

A voice speaks low, and somewhat quivery. 'Yes, a ghost.'

This is so wonderful; Bella would leap up toward the ceiling in excitement, but her leaping days are long gone. She claps her hands instead.

She seats herself on a satin-covered vanity bench and crosses her legs, settling in for a long conversation. 'So how many years have you been haunting Izzy's bathroom?'

The low voice says, 'A very, very long time.'

'Does Izzy know about you?'

'No, I'm a secret.' He waves his arms in various directions, imitating his idea of something spiritual. 'But it will be dark soon and you must leave before the witching hour. Tell no one about me or you die. Leave now!'

Bella leaps up, hands pointed upward, as in prayer, 'So sorry, so sorry. Leaving!'

With that she's out in the corridor and stumbling for the staircase, lickety-split.

Downstairs, she pulls at Sophie. 'Let's go, *now*.'

'I haven't watered the plants yet.'

'Never mind. We gotta get outa here. This place is haunted!'

Bella muses, as she runs; 'what a stud. If I was only fifty years younger. And if he wasn't dead . . .'

'What are you mumbling about?'

Bella only smiles.

Thirty-One
Moments After Bella Runs

Dix drops his towel, pulls on a pair of jeans over his wet, naked body, laughing and scratching, as the shower curtain draws open and Hicks and Dockson, damp frowning twins in black suits, leap out of the tub with guns drawn.

'This is the most fun I've had since, well, heck, who even remembers. I can't believe you guys jumped into the shower to hide! Dummies!'

Dockson is annoyed. 'Where the hell were we gonna hide when she was already at the door? You had to call us in while you were taking a shower? What for?'

Ignoring him. 'You should have seen the old broad's face when she thought I was a ghost. And then turned scaredy-cat when I told her I'd kill her if she told anybody.' More side-splitting laughter from Dix.

'Who the hell was that looney-toon?' Hicks wants to know, pocketing his weapon, in his wet pants, and reaching for a towel. 'What was she doing in your father's house? She knew where the key was hidden.'

'Who knows? Who cares?'

'But what if she comes back? We should have offed her,' adds Dockson, grabbing Hicks's towel and wiping his soggy face.

'You two are always so quick with the offing. Maybe she's just a sweet old lady.' Hicks frowns. 'Always with the guns. And killing.'

Dockson and Dix ignore Hicks; to them he's the wussy of the three.

'Nah. Too messy. And what would we do with the body?' Dix finishes dressing and heads for the stairs. The other two follow, flapping their arms in an attempt to get dry.

'It was the steam; she thought I was a spirit. I shoulda dropped my towel and given her a cheap thrill.'

His buddies laugh.

'Or you guys coulda pop your heads out of the curtain, woulda give you a hell of a guffaw. And probably give her a heart attack.'

'What about that other dame downstairs? What if she tells her?' says Hicks, worry-wart, again.

'Bet ya fifty bucks you're wrong. She was so strung out, she'll be lucky if she remembers her name.'

Hicks is shocked. 'Old dame like that doin' drugs. What's the world coming to?'

They are in the living room now, searching drawers and cupboards. Dockson holds up a half-bottle of sweet sherry. 'This all the booze your pop has? Pathetic.'

'So take my pop's car out of the garage and go find a liquor store. I love that the guy leaves the keys in his amazing expensive car.'

Hicks worries some more. 'Drive an antique Edsel around? Wouldn't that make us stick out like a sore thumb?'

'They'll assume he's in it. And, by the by, you think we're gonna leave that beauty here when we go? Not a chance. A special extra gift from dear old Dad.'

'And what about your dad? How come he isn't in that car out somewheres? Where is he? What if he walks in?' asks Dockson.

'So, like I said, I give him a great big hug and sloppy kiss and say, "Glad to see your sonny boy again?" He'll be thrilled. Will you stop with the maybes? We got a perfect setup. The SUV is hidden. A great hidey-hole to do our job from here. Never thought the old guy would be of any use to me, and now he will be, whether I have to kill him later or not.'

'Maybe,' hopes Hicks, that less bloody-driven partner, 'he's away on some vacation and we'll be in and out before he gets back.'

Dockson is also concerned. 'What about nosy neighbors? This layout is almost too good to be true.'

'Hey, scram; why don't you go and pick up some groceries along with the booze and leave the big thinking to me. I can't wait to sleep in my old room again. I wonder if he saved my old baseball cards.'

On his way out, Dockson pauses at the baby grand piano and picks up the father-son photo. 'That you, as a kid?'

'That's me, buck teeth and all. Hated the buzzard even then. If I could have run away at nine, I would have.'

'Why? Did he beat on you?'

'Nah. He was just some wimpy guy. A nobody.'

'So,' asks Dockson, 'what's the story? Must be a story, if you already knew you wanted to jump ship at nine.'

'What do ya wanna know for? You hate your daddy-o, too?'

Dockson. 'Never knew mine. My pop was hit and run. Knock her up and leave town.'

They laugh.

'What about you, Hicks?'

'My daddy was a wife-beater. Maybe they named that undershirt after him.'

They all laugh again.

Hicks, pressing now, 'Yours must have done

183

something that made you wanna leave these rich, fancy digs. What are you hiding?'

'I'm not hiding anything. You really need to hear this dull stuff?'

'What else have we got to do until we grab the girl? Entertain us.'

'Grandpa made his dough in the stock market, which bought him this mansion and plenty more. My father just pissed most of it away. He was always full of grandiose plans. I'm gonna do this. Build this. Buy this. Fix this. I'm gonna be a big shot. Talk. Talk. Talk. Everything he touched turned to zilch. After rich Grandpa died, my brilliant dad wanted to sell the house, so we could go to some desert isle and drink Mai Tais. It was damned lucky that Mom talked him out of that or we would have ended up living in the streets. He wanted to be someone important; he was waiting for an inspiration that never came; he was a nothing, a dumb dreamer.'

Hicks and Dockson exchange glances. This is the most they ever heard out of their leader, Dix.

Hicks keeps picking at the sore, while Dockson listens nervously. In his mind, Dix is like a pit bull. You don't poke at him. Or he bites. But Hicks pushes on. 'I'm not hearing a reason for you leaving.'

For a moment, Dix does look ready to snarl, but he's caught up in his own recollections. 'My mother made plans to leave him; she was gonna take me with her. I was thrilled, because I was glad to be rid of dear daddy, who I thought was a loser, and who wasn't exactly crazy about me. I even packed a suitcase and hid it under

184

my bed. But one day I woke up and she was gone. Hey, Mom, I wanted to call after her; you forgot something. Me. I cried for days.'

'What did you father say?' asks Dockson.

'What did he say when he realized she was gone? He looked at me in surprise, and asked, 'You still here?' From then on he treated me like I was wallpaper.

Dockson primed, as if ready to race out of the room if Dix blew a gasket.

But Dix was still in his past. 'My dad decided that Mom had had a good idea and he took off, too. My signal to take off.'

Dockson looks surprised. In spite of his fear, he blurts, 'You ran away at nine?'

A sly smile from Dix. 'No, by then I was thirteen and I was as disgusted with him as he was with himself. That's when I left and hitched my way across the country, as far away as I could get from him.'

The partners' eyes fix on everywhere but at him. Waiting for Dix to fly into a rage.

Dix growls; he's sorry he let them see him weak. None of their damn business. 'Go on, get outta here and pick up the groceries. And be careful with Daddy's car. It's worth a small fortune.'

They run.

Part Seven
The Capture

Thirty-Two
The Mall – Shop Till You Drop

I expected this shopping excursion at Sawgrass Mills Mall would be unpleasant. I wanted to have buffers against Tori's expected obnoxious behavior. I had hoped Evvie could join us. No luck; she and Joe had tickets to a play matinée. Bella and Sophie were off somewhere, being very mysterious about it. Only one person left to ask. My Jack. It won't be easy, since I still haven't told Jack about Ida's 'confession'. I keep waiting for the right time. However, this isn't it. Why have I been stalling? I don't know. But anyway, here goes.

I find him in our sun room. In shorts and a tee shirt. His bare feet are up high, leaning on the railing. A cold beer and sandwich are on the small patio table near him. He looks so comfortable. Too relaxed, not a good sign.

I put my arms around his neck from behind him and nuzzle his ear. 'Comfy?' I ask sweetly.

'Sure am.'

'You know where I'm going today?'

'Heard some rumor about shopping with the girls. Ida is taking Tori to the mall because she needs a new outfit. Our Hy promises to take her out to the track, amazing as that sounds.' He laughs. 'The *Yenta* machine doles out local news bulletins daily. No fake news for them.'

'You heard right.'

I take a deep breath before I plunge in. 'Well, you know how it is between Ida and Tori. Chalk and cheese. So, I'm going with them to keep this little volcano from erupting.' Why am I making light of it?

'How brave of you.'

I am rubbing his neck. I hear a few happy moans in return.

A quick blurt, 'So, I was thinking you might want to come along.' I hold my breath. 'And help out.'

'You know I was planning to watch a Dolphins game on TV today with Morrie, at his place.'

'Yes, but I was hoping . . .'

He turns around; my arms drop from his neck. He lifts up both of his hands; I assume he's pretending they are scales. 'Let me see, I'll weigh my options here.' He lifts one hand, as if lifting something light. 'A happy time with my son, and other guys; his cop pals. Lots of beer and cheering or booing the game, as the case may be. Hearing cop jokes, trading stories and lots of laughing. Or . . .' His other hand drops like a stone. 'Spend my precious hours with a spoiled brat, bent on making everyone miserable.' He keeps pretending to weigh his options. Up and down. Up and down. Hiding a smile; he's enjoying toying with me.

'Stop that,' I say. Hiding my own smile. He's

190

so adorable. I know I've lost this battle, but he's so much fun to watch.

'I rest my case.' Naturally, we kiss.

So, I am stuck with the job of referee between unhappy Grandma Ida and rebellious grandchild, Tori; not my favorite idea of spending an afternoon. And Jack is unaware of the severity of their situation. So, I am on my own. Oh, well, grin and bear it.

This is a pretty section of Bloomingdale's outlet store. In one corner there is a black baby grand piano. A stately looking woman, her straight blonde hair in a chignon, dressed in severe black with a white collar at her throat, is seated there, playing Chopin études. The music is sweet and relaxing.

And adjoining her is a colorful rainbow fountain, with constantly lit flowing water pouring down from a small marble statue at its center; Eros, the god of Love, with bow-and-arrow poised.

We are nearby in the teen department of Bloomingdale's, looking at skirts for Tori to wear for when (and if) she goes with Hy on the promised trip to Hialeah racetrack.

Ida holds up a skirt that is three inches below the knee. We've already given up on dresses. This is her eighth attempt at pleasing the princess. 'It's a flared skirt, something modern,' touts Ida.

'It's a skirt for old ladies, like you. Pass.'

Another Ida selection. A charming floral pattern of daisies. Tori gives her opinion of that choice.

She places her forefinger inside her throat, making a gagging motion, and turns away. Snarky at every turn.

Ida hangs it back up on the rack. 'You have to pick something. And stop looking at dungarees!'

Tori practically spits. 'They're called jeans. They're denims. They're skinny jeans. They're Wrangler's. Or chinos. They're designer jeans, or blue jeans. I wouldn't be caught dead wearing *dungarees*!'

I try to calm her. 'Well, it came originally from the word *dungeree* in the year 1600 from the Hindi *dungri* meaning coarse cotton.' Years of being a librarian filled my brain full of usually useless information like this. 'In America, Levi Strauss, a miner—'

Tori swats at me to shut up. 'Dungarees! Dung! Comes from shit!'

Ida lifts her hand to slap her, but stops herself. 'If we were at home, I'd wash your mouth out with soap.'

Tori shoots her down with disdain. 'Again, you and your soap-mouth washings. It's not my home! Get a life!'

Ida backs up as if she'd been smacked. She moves away from us. If there was a corner to hide in, that's where she'd be.

Tori ignores her and holds up a plain blue skirt for me to approve.

I shake my head. 'I'm not sure they'd even accept anything in denim at the Turf Club gate.' I am still sticking to the 'dress code' as if it were the rule throughout Hialeah. Jack had laughed when I told him about my little fib. He'd called it a downright lie, and what kind of woman was his wife becoming?

Ida looks like she might faint. I get her to sit down on a small couch. She does so, takes out a handkerchief to use as a fan. I indicate that she should rest and I'll take over.

It takes a while until Tori finds something barely acceptable. It's another flared skirt, but it's knee-length. We find a cotton top that sort of matches, according to the fashion rules of Tori, and we are finally done.

At checkout, Tori takes money from her pouch. Ida pulls herself up from the couch and lifts out her wallet. 'Let me buy this for you. Think of it as a birthday present.'

'I can buy my own clothes.' She glares at Ida, who tries to hold back her cries of despair. 'I changed my mind. Yeah, you pay for it. Won't make up for all the years of birthday presents I never got from you.'

Another knife-stab to Ida's heart.

I've had enough. While we wait for the packages to be wrapped, I face the two adversaries. 'Isn't it about time to make peace? What will it take to stop this needless, unending war?'

Ida jumps at the chance. 'Yes, please. Tori I'm so sorry. Let me apologize. For everything.'

Tori says, 'Not so fast, Grandma. You don't get off so easy.' Tori remains rigid, with arms locked tight.

She turns to me. 'You want us to stop the war. Who asked you to stick your nose in my business? Stick to your own stupid business. Mrs Perfect: what do you know about pain and misery? You have a pretty-boy husband. You get to tell all your old lady friends what they should do, and when you say jump they jump.'

Ida says weakly, 'Gladdy is my friend; she's just trying to help.'

'Well, let her go rescue some old biddy who fell in her bathtub. Tell her to stay out of my life.'

'Stop it! You don't know what you're talking about.' Ida looks to me, chagrined. She knows my own heartbreak and she feels this child has no right to attack me.

'It's all right, Ida. Don't worry about me.' I turn to Tori. 'Hate gets you nowhere.'

'I'm good at hate. It's what I do best.'

'But you're letting it define you.' Soothing tone; I try to calm her down. 'Everybody gets hurt sometime in their lives. I'm not belittling your pain, but how long do you need to hold on to this hate? When you hate someone, you are the one who suffers. It ruins your life. It stops you from ever being happy, or feeling joy, or having a healthy life.'

Tori covers her ears with her hands. 'Bla-bla-bla,' she says to shut me out.

I give up. I'm a failure at negotiating.

By now the people who have been walking by have stopped and are gaping at us. Even the pianist watches us act out our family drama as she continues to play. She switches to a funeral dirge – her musical comment on our situation. I wonder who else in the crowd gets it.

There is even one insensitive young guy who

194

has been circling us, shooting a video with his iPhone. Perhaps he thinks it's an incident that will get him many 'likes' on his Facebook page. 'Get away, pest!'

He ignores me. When he points his phone at us, Ida and I automatically look away from him.

Not our Tori, not in-your-face Tori. 'Hey, you, pig boy . . .' she calls, heading toward him, blood in her eyes.

He startles, but only for a moment. Up close, he seems younger, maybe not even twenty. He grins as she approaches and quickly presses the snapshot button, taking rat-a-tat shot after shot of her.

'Cut that out!' demands tough Tori. 'Or you'll live to regret it!'

He circles around her, continuing to 'shoot'. 'You can't stop me. It's a free country.'

'Oh, can't I? What about my right to privacy!?' She tries to grab at the phone, but he keeps the dancing around, holding the camera high. He laughs as he says, 'This week, my subject is *Mean Girls*, and you are the meanest girl I've ever shot!'

The guy is way taller than Tori and she is getting nowhere, trying to reach his hand.

But what's this? Is it a bird? Is it a plane! It's Superwoman, come to save the day! (Or was that Mighty Mouse?) There's Ida racing towards the two of them, as if she does have wings. She practically leaps into the camera guy, shoving him with all her old-lady strength. And with an impressive jab to his middle, he falls backward – into the fountain. Landing next to Eros, seeing his iPhone drown!

195

Ida shrieks, with fists ready to cause more damage. 'Nobody gets to call my granddaughter "mean"!'

The guy wails, soaking wet, digging around the water desperately. 'You ruined my phone . . . my camera!'

To my utter amazement, Tori grabs Ida and whirls her around, hugging her. 'I love you, Grandma. I do!'

'I love you, too, baby. Can you forgive me?'

The melting tough girl, 'I forgive you. I do. I do.'

'If I could take it all back . . . I did everything wrong. I never should have left you.'

'You don't have to explain. I understand. You did what you had to do. You had to take care of Grandpa Murray.'

Ida, sadly, 'It didn't help. He died anyway.' She pauses, remembering. 'I never wanted to leave you; you were the sweetest, most adorable baby. I just was so guilt-ridden about what I did to your mom. I ruined everybody's lives. You have a right to hate me. I hate myself.'

'I know. I know. You don't have to hate your-self anymore.'

They walk toward me, arm in arm.

I am stunned. What's just happened? They're still at it, blubbering together.

'I'm so sorry, that I left you to the Steiners. They never got over losing Fred.'

'They weren't so bad . . .'

'Yes, they were.'

She grins. 'Yes, they were, and she was such an awful cook.'

'Remember those awful smoked beer sausages; she burnt them every time.'

196

They both laugh.

The guy in the fountain mutters, 'Just lost the best shot of the day.'

Tori grabs the packages. 'Let's get the heck out of here.'

With a background of a crowd applauding us, we three take bows and, with what's left of our dignity, we exit the store.

I have no idea what made this amazing shift in that girl, but I'll pretend my little speech had something to do with it.

Thirty-Three
An Unexpected Stop

By the time we reach the exit of the mall, Tori and Ida are still holding hands and grinning happily at one another. Ida suddenly stops. 'Wait. I need to go back. I have to use the rest room.'

'Okay,' I say, 'we'll wait right here for you.'

'Don't bother. The bathrooms are way back toward the center. It'll take me a while. I'll meet you back at the car.'

'Okay, definitely back at the car.'

Once she hobbles off, I turn to Tori. 'Do you want to make a quick stop for a soda? Or a snack? We can stall going out in the heat.'

'No, it's really stuffy in here. Let's just get to the car. We can turn on the AC if we want. Right now, for a few minutes, I'd like some real air.'

197

'All right.'

Tori swings the handles of her clothing packages in a jolly fashion.

I'm still walking on air with what just happened. I feel like Winston Churchill must have felt when his impassioned speeches helped Britain win the war against Germany.

Ida has conversations with herself as she hurries down the wide aisles of the massive mall. Why am I rushing? Because I want to get back to Tori. There's so much more I want to say to her. I'm so happy. She doesn't hate me anymore . . . oops, wait, I think I have to make a left.

I'm trying to find the Nike store. I remember from previous times, there was a bathroom in there. I also remember us always complaining that there were so few bathrooms in this huge place, and somebody should do something about it. There was some lady on Google wrote about it, that they were poorly marked and hard for seniors to find. No use thinking about that just now. Why couldn't I just wait till we got home? Well, some things can't be held back. I giggle. Was Nike near a Bed, Bath and Beyond? I don't think so. But something tells me I'd better walk faster. Thank goodness, I see Nike way down at that end. I wish I had worn more comfortable shoes. My feet are killing me. Maybe I should buy a pair when I'm in Nike. Not that they'd carry the kind of shoes I would wear. It's a store for kids. Or people with bad taste. Never mind, thank God, here's the store.

I keep trying to find the bathroom. I have no idea where in the store it is. All I see are shoes and boots. But I do see lots of sneakers; they look nice . . . no, forget it, I have no time to shop. I try to find a sales clerk so I can ask where the bathroom is. Rots-a-ruck with that. Finding employees is like finding hens' teeth. Impossible. Oh, goody, never mind, I see it down in that corner right near a dressing room. I practically hop and skip getting there. I *need* to get there fast now.

What's this? There's some kind of mop in a sudsy bucket barring the door. Never mind, I can walk around it.

'You can't come in here!' A harsh voice from inside calls out to me. I keep going and I turn and enter the bathroom itself.

'I said, stay out!' The voice is coming from a woman, who stands eight feet tall, huge-bellied with green and gray hair and sweeping up the floor. Eight feet – I know that's an exaggeration, but that's how I see her. She has a cigarette dangling from her lips. Isn't there a law against smoking in the whole mall? Never mind that. Never mind how she looks. I have something more important to worry about. My bladder! My unhappy, complaining bladder!

'I'm cleaning up in here. You have to wait outside till I'm through,' the Amazon shouts.

'But . . . but . . . I have to go!' I'm about to rush past her and zoom into one of the cubicles, but I picture her breaking the door down and dragging me out by my hair. I really should stop watching late-night TV vampire movies.

The huge woman drops the broom and picks up a long-handled thick black brush and comes

199

after me, shooing me out of the room. 'Yeah – go to one of the other toilets in some other store.'

'Which stores are they?'

'How the hell am I supposed to know? What do you think I am, some social director?'

'But you clean the bathrooms? You should know where they are.' Why am I debating with a lunatic? I wanna smack her. But she'd probably kill me with one blow. Or throw Febreze in my face.

I'm wasting time. I have to find another bathroom. Fast.

I trot down the middle row looking every which way. I pass TK Maxx. Somehow I doubt they have a bathroom. Too cheap to build one. How about that kiddy clothing store? Nah, the toilet seats are only for three-year olds.

Past the Target store. Wait. I need a new potato-peeler, maybe I should go in . . . No, are you crazy? Okay, now we're on the ball – here's the rich stores. Saks Fifth Avenue and Ralph Lauren. They'd make sure there are toilets for their rich lady shoppers. And high enough so they can get out of them. But I look a sweaty mess by now. They probably would stick up their noses and ignore me. I pass.

Three more right and left turns. I give up. So, mind over bladder. I've told my bladder it just has to wait.

I race for the exit and I hope I can find it before I grow another year older.

Gladdy and Tori must be so annoyed waiting outside in that hot sun.

Thirty-Four

Something Wicked this way Comes

When we arrive out on the street I locate my Chevy wagon. I'm ahead of Tori. She's stopped to listen to messages on her phone. I'm sure she's keeping her distance, so I won't know who she's talking to. Still Ms Secretive.

I reach my car, open the door, and climb inside quickly for a minute to turn on the air. The seats are too hot for us to get in just yet. I need to cool the car. Leaving the keys in the ignition, I get back out quickly.

Then, I look around, perturbed. I'm aware that there's another car, double-parked, blocking me. It's a black SUV with tinted-glass windows. I can't tell who is inside. Surely they'll move, now that they see I need to pull out.

I leave the sidewalk and stand in the gutter for a moment, sending hand signals to the car that is blocking us. But they don't seem to notice.

I squeeze in between my vehicle and the car in front, then head for the driver's side of the offending auto to suggest politely that they move on.

I hear Tori catching up to me. As I reach the

SUV, I hear her shout. 'No! Get back! Get back! Get away from them!'

For a moment, I think I'm imagining things. But, no, she is suddenly running toward me and yelling. She drops her packages; they land in the gutter.

The things I notice, even under stress; something odd is happening; a man jumps out of the passenger-side front seat of the SUV. To my amazement, he's holding a gun, which he's holding low, so it won't be seen by others. It's not a very big gun, but a gun is a gun. He's a bulky man wearing a three-piece suit – in this heat!

Where is that guy with the iPhone camera when we need him? He could get this for the police. Tori is waving her arms now. What on earth is going on?

The man grabs me around my waist. I try to pull away, but he grips me harder. Despite my shock, my mind is racing; I try to think of what to do, but there's no time. In a moment I'm forced into the back seat of the SUV, where another man waits to grab me and slap duct tape over my mouth. Duct tape? Really? Like in the movies? What madness is this?

From inside the car, I look out to see Tori hesitating. Don't do it, I say to her in my mind. Forget about me. Get away. Save yourself! What to do? She foolishly wants to come to help me. But whoever these men are, they are serious and fast. In seconds, two men are already at her side. Tori is kicking as one of the men grabs her and the other one holds his hand over her mouth. They are doing this low down, to keep from being seen.

Tori is tossed into the car, landing almost on top of me.

She has only one moment to shout, 'Dix, you bastard,' before her mouth is clamped shut with duct tape, too. I look at Tori and her eyes reflect terror.

The man called Dix answers, 'Told you we'd meet again, honey bunch.'

In moments, blindfolds cover our eyes, and in seconds, we are being driven away from the mall. Surely someone heard Tori scream. And witnessed us being pulled into the SUV? Is anyone dialing 911? I hope so.

I get it right away. Tori hadn't been lying. She knows these men. There *were* men who were coming after her. Men threatening to kill her. Why didn't she let us know this was serious? Why? I suddenly feel chilled and it isn't just from the air-conditioning.

Ida exits the mall and heads directly to Gladdy's car. She feels guilty that she took so long. Wait till she tells them her frustrating bathroom adventure. They'll laugh. She reaches the car where it is parked, but Gladdy and Tori are nowhere in sight. Looking around, she is puzzled. Where could they be in this heat? Surely they didn't go back to the mall. But if they had, Gladdy would have phoned to tell her. It's unlike Gladdy not to be where she said she would be.

Then Ida notices the car door is open. She moves to it slowly, getting a bad feeling about it. She looks inside and sees, to her shock, the keys are turned on in the ignition. The car is cold. Something's wrong. Very wrong.

Ida glances again up and down the street, nervous now. Then her eye is caught by something else. In the gutter are Tori's Bloomingdale's packages! Now open, with the newly bought outfit half fallen out of its box. It takes a moment for it to register.

Then, Ida screams.

Thirty-Five
Kidnapped

Jack and Morrie try to calm Ida. But she just keeps blubbering. 'I was only gone a little while. Where could they be? What could have happened?' She tugs at Morrie's arm. 'Look at her clothes in the gutter! I left them there for you to see. You're a policeman, do something!'

The streets are full of shoppers and shoppers-to-be. Mall shopping always brings a big crowd. Jack and Morrie look around, stopping and talking to people in the vicinity, as to whether they saw or heard anything. No luck.

A car pulls up to where they are standing in the middle of the street. A young female shopper rolls down her window. They can see her back seat is full of packages with mall-store labels. 'Is there a problem?'

While Ida continues to moan, Jack briefly

describes what Gladdy and Tori look like. The shopper says, 'I might have seen something, though at the time I didn't think anything about it. An older woman and a young girl came along and it seemed like there was one car and another one double-parked parallel to it. They headed for the double-parked car and two men came out of the car to help them in, so I guessed that these were husbands or boyfriends waiting who couldn't find anyplace to park. They were in a rush, it seemed, and they sort of hurried the women in and drove away quickly. I assumed they didn't want to be ticketed. Is it possible, these are the people you are looking for?'

Jack asks, 'Can you describe the men?'

She shakes her head. 'Just guys, maybe in their forties, but, honestly, I didn't really look at them. I was busy trying to extricate my car from a way-too-tight parking space. It took me a sweaty while.' She smiles.

Morrie asks, 'What kind of car was it?'

'It was an SUV like mine.' She indicates her dark forest green vehicle. 'Only theirs was black.'

Ida looks terrified at that.

Jack cautiously asks, 'Did you happen to notice the license number?'

'Well, why would I? It seemed harmless.' She gasps, suddenly realizing. 'Oh, my God, no I didn't. Are they in trouble?'

They don't answer her question. Morrie thanks her for stopping and giving them her information. Jack and Morrie exchange worried glances. Ida is moaning.

The woman starts to drive away, than backs up. 'I did notice one thing. The license plate wasn't Florida. They were California's colors. I once lived there and I recognized that.'

They thank her again.

Jack swears angrily, and meets his son's agreeing eyes. 'A black SUV: where have we heard that before?'

Ida is beside herself. 'Somebody kidnapped them! It's the killers she told us about. They'll murder them!' Ida is about to faint and Morrie catches her in time.

Ida cries, 'If I only hadn't gone back to find a bathroom. And then I got lost and couldn't find the exit again. I was away such a long time. Maybe if we had stayed together, we might have been gone before these men came.'

Jack tries to comfort her. 'You don't know that. You might have been taken, too.' He doesn't mention how it might have been worse. If these men felt threatened by her, he shudders to think what they might have done. He knew his Gladdy would have kept calm. This woman turns easily hysterical. But there's no sense her feeling guilty. Gladdy wouldn't want that.

Jack senses he's kidding himself, trying to hide his own guilt. He's ashamed now that he made fun of them going shopping. If only he had come along, as Gladdy had asked. He smiles grimly at the irony. He needs to give himself the same advice he gave Ida. Feeling guilty doesn't help anything.

He will find those men and when he does . . .

Thirty-Six
The Hideout

The two guys (not the driver) shove us out of the SUV. We are in some garage; I can tell by the smell of gasoline. I hear a door being unlocked into some room. Once they bring us inside the room, blindfolds and duct tape are removed. And immediately Tori gives them hell. 'Where's that piece of crap Dix? That coward!'

One of the men tries for a leer; I note he's not very good at playing tough guy. The other one is also uncomfortable. That's interesting, something to remember. 'Don't worry, babe,' he says weakly, 'you'll be seeing him plenty. You better have some answers for him. Or else.'

'Or else, what, you moron?'

She knows these men. She met them on the road. But she knew them even before that. Where? What in her past could be so dangerous, that we are possibly about to lose our lives? One thing I'm sure of – I'd better focus. We have to find our way out of this mess. Oh, Jack, my darling. He will be so worried for me. He'll try to find us. But will he be in time?

Tori turns to me, pointing. 'Say hello to Dockson and Hicks. These dumb apes work for Chaz Dix.'

Dix? Why does that name sound familiar? I keep hoping this is some sick joke.

Hicks tries to play tough guy. 'Okay, gimme your purses, and both of you empty your pockets.' He looks through them, checks each item off, tossing every bit of equipment into a paper bag. 'iPhone. Check.' He looks at me, holding another phone up. 'What's this old thing? Some toy?'

I get huffy. 'It's *my* phone. My flip-top phone. It works just fine. Like to see how I use it?' I reach out. He pulls away, grinning.

Both guys chortle at my antique. 'I don't think so.'

'Shucks,' I say.

Tori empties her denim jacket pockets and Hy's racetrack program falls out onto the floor. Hicks picks it up and smiles. 'You a gambler, like to lose money at the track, girly?'

Tori grabs for it, but he holds it out of reach, then turns the first page.

'Won the first two races, lucky girl. Temple Star and Glory Girl.' He shoves it in the bag holding all our personal belongings.

Tori grabs at his arm. 'Give that back to me!'

'What for?' Dockson says. 'That program is long over.'

'A friend gave it to me. I want it back!'

They are leaving. I act goofy and play at funny. 'Be nice, guys, her boyfriend gave it to her. Hey, counting horses at night is better than counting sheep, right?' I force myself into a silly grin.

A moment as they think about it, then Hicks tosses it back to her. 'Happy dreams,' he says. They start out.

'Hey, wait one damn minute!' Tori quickly looks around; she yells out at them, 'Where are we supposed to pee!'

But she's talking to a wall. A metal wall. The whole room is metal. They're gone and we can hear the bolt closing us off from the other side.

I shake my head, impressed. 'You millennials are tough.'

Now defeated, Tori says, 'Yeah, me and my big mouth have got us into a load of crap. Sorry.' She laughs. 'My *boyfriend?* Dorky old Hy? An old racetrack program? That was really funny. How come you pulled that?'

'Because you wanted it and I wanted to test how tough they really are.' Tori puts the useless program back in her pocket. 'Maybe we can tear the pages and make paper guns to attack them with.' We both manage to laugh.

'So Dix is the leader; the others are soft. It may help us later.'

We walk the room.

'We're doomed. Dix won't get anything he wants from me and we're dead meat.'

'Okay, shove the panic aside and let's use our brains and see what we can do for ourselves, until we are rescued.'

'Yeah, right. Rescued. By your husband, the cop, where he'll find two dead bodies.'

'Stop that! It's not constructive. Here's what we know so far. We rode in the car for twenty minutes, and we are not that far from where I live. I guess that because I heard fire trucks go by and I know the street where the station is. We are in a residential area; at least they didn't take us out of town. I heard children playing. An ice-cream truck rang its bells. Finally we were driven up what I thought at first was a hill, but it was too short for that. The ground under it was gravel or concrete so I assumed it's a driveway. For a moment, I smelled something, from out the window – some kind of plant in a garden, maybe? The aroma is familiar, but I can't place it.

'We then entered what I'm sure is a garage, where we were pulled out of the car. Then, immediately, we were taken into this room, so I'm guessing, since we didn't feel any weather change, this room is attached to the garage.'

We continue to walk around, inspecting every corner, including the ceiling. 'Now look around with me. We are in a structure not too much larger than the average garage. It is totally made of metal and there is no exit except for that small door in the back, which of course is now locked.'

'Wow,' says Tori. 'You're like some power PI. I'm impressed.'

'You forget we are private investigators and that includes your grandmother.'

'Grandma Ida, also?'

'Yes, she's an important member. Pay attention; we need to figure out what, if anything, we can do to get out of here. And speaking of Ida, these men are assuming I am your grandmother. Do not tell them who I am.'

'Why not?' This amuses Tori. She says, kindly teasing, 'You want to snivel every minute?'

'Their not knowing may be useful.'

Tori frowns, gloomy now. 'We'll never get out of here alive.'

210

'Let's not go there again. Pay attention. This is an empty kind of work shed. You can see where they tore down any shelving that was once here. There are plug outlets, so lamps or machinery were here once. Alas, no windows. So, I guess we are in a metal shed connected to a garage behind someone's house.'

'Maybe if we yell someone will hear us.'

'I doubt it. There isn't anything we can use to bang on the metal walls.'

'It's hopeless.' Tori strides from wall to wall, hitting the metal with her fists.

'Don't bother. I imagine that the real owners are away. Banging will only irritate your "Dicks or Dix", as you call him, and we don't need that. We have one advantage and you hit on it.'

'I did?'

'There's no bathroom in here. No porta-potty, which means they didn't think this through to provide everything. Maybe because they arrived here only days ago, the men who followed you from California. They'll have to take us to a bathroom in the house.'

'I hope they're civilized enough to do that,' Tori says, still negative.

'They were civilized enough to give us two sleeping bags to sit and sleep on, so let's hope for the best.'

There is also a disadvantage. It's stuffy in here, with no fresh air. The shed holds the heat and it's uncomfortably warm. I'm sweating already. It's late afternoon and it will start to cool down by evening. But what will it be like at high noon? Worry about it tomorrow.

With that, I slide downward and seat myself on one of the sleeping bags. 'And don't forget we have my husband and his son who will find us. Yes, they will. But first sit down and tell me everything you know about these guys and what they want and why they grabbed you. Tori, it's about time for the truth.'

Tori drops down onto her sleeping bag to join me, and, with no hope, finally starts to tell me the whole story.

'I came here to find my father,' she begins . . .

Thirty-Seven
Meanwhile, Back at the Ranch

Jack is holding court in his and Gladdy's apartment. Morrie has called in to his precinct an APB to find a black SUV with California plates.

It's quite a collection as they are seated on couches, chairs and the floor of the living room. The four girls – Sophie and Bella just recently returned from feeding the goldfish. Ida, still in a frenzy; and Evvie, the only sane one in a motley group of hysterical hand-wringers. And, of course, Evvie's husband, Joe. Plus Hy, who insists he wants to help; he's already become attached to Tori. Which means, also in attendance, his shadow wife, Lola. Hy defers to Jack, the professional.

So, unlike his usual self-serving self, he stays quiet, for the most part. Others wanted in, but Jack held them down to these seven.

They've already heard Ida tell the kidnap story at least seven times. With accompanying tears and cries of dismay. They've also had tea (with cookies), another necessity, and now, frightened and wide-eyed, they pay attention. Jack must marshal his troops. 'So far, what we can guess is that three men followed Tori from California to here. Joe remembers that Tori spoke about running into these men when she was in New Mexico.'

Ida sobs out, 'Those men want to kill her. That's what she said when we met her at the deli!' She shudders, 'And poor Gladdy . . .'

Joe adds, 'But Tori didn't tell us why these men were chasing her. She obviously knew them.'

Jack sighs, points at the girls. 'Promise – no more frantic outbursts. We have to put our heads together and think clearly. We have to figure out why she came here and why she was in danger from these men. We found out she was looking for a couple named Harvey and Lila Woodley. Why them? We know she had a photo of the Woodleys with her mother and dad at their wedding thirty years ago.'

Hy raises his hand. Then drops it. 'Sorry. That name sounds familiar to me.' He shakes his head. 'But I don't know why.' Lola pats her hubby on his back. 'You'll remember soon, sweetness, you always do.'

Evvie speaks. 'Remember when she said she

met these three guys, she called them Hickory, Dickory, Doc? It was a play on their names.'

Sophie giggles. 'She called one of them a dick.'

Bella looks confused. She doesn't know why that's funny.

Evvie says, 'But I heard that name as Dicks. And why does that name sound familiar?'

Evvie and Hy exchange frustrated glances. Their memory is not functioning today. It's always the nouns that get forgotten in later age. They remember Gladdy used to say that all the time – the nouns are the first to go.

Jack says, 'I am going to get in touch with Tori's sisters. I hope they'll know something. Ida, I need their names and if you know how to reach them.'

Ida is miserable. 'The girls are married. I don't know their married names.' She hides her head in shame; how can she not know anything about her other grandchildren? Or even her great-grandchildren?

'That's why we have Morrie, here.'

Morrie nods. 'I'm available 24/7. Call and tell me or Jack anything you remember. Any info. Names. City. Streets. I'll be able to track them down.'

Jack stands up. 'Okay, go on home, but everybody think hard. You might know something you don't realize is important. Even if it sounds silly, tell us anyway.'

As they pile out, they each stop to say kind words to Jack.

Evvie is the last to leave. Sister and brother-in-law hug.

'We'll find her, Ev,' Jack promises.

'I know we will.'

They both know the words are kind, but meaningless.

When Jack is alone, he sits down, head in his hands. Now he allows himself to show how tense and worried he really feels.

Gladdy, where are you?

Thirty-Eight
The Tough Guys

It isn't too long until the guys come back into the shed. Dockson and Hicks bring snacks and drinks which they place beside Gladdy and Tori, still seated on the floor. Dix glares at them.

Tori pushes the food away. 'Thanks for nothing, you dummies.'

I sigh. That brave girl doesn't know how to keep her emotions to herself.

The leader, Dix, turns to me. 'Tell your granddaughter to keep her trap shut.'

Tori almost forgets. 'She's not . . .' then stops herself.

Dix is interested. 'Finish your sentence. Your grandmother, what? What does she not . . .?'

Tori straightens up, looks at me. 'You're wasting your time. Grandma does *not* know anything about anything. I told you that a million times!'

I nod at her. Good girl, she remembered.

'Okay, let's get down to it again and again. Where's Daddy?'

'You can ask me till you're blue in the face, I don't know. I didn't know in LA or New Mexico, and I still don't know. I've been trying to find him, but with no luck.'

'I don't believe you.' He turns to me. 'Come on, Grandma, surely your son-in-law would have contacted you if he lived here. You would have cried together about his poor wifey, still in the pokey.'

I put on a counterfeit pathetic face and sniveling voice. 'Don't I wish he had, but he hated me. I was the one who turned him in to the cops.' I wipe away fake tears, and phony sadness. Playing the distraught grandma, I play falsely eager. 'Do you really think he's here? That darling boy, oh how I've missed him. If you find Freddy, tell him I'm so sorry.'

It works. Dix now thinks I'm stupid and useless. The irony is not lost on me. I've been imitating Ida.

Tori pleads. 'Listen to me. I know I'm on a wild-goose chase. My dad's dead, my mom's in prison. My other grandparents just died. I have nobody. I came here because I'm going to live with my dear Florida Grandmother Ida . . .' And here she gives me a clumsy attempt at a hug.

Dix grins. 'Nice try, babe. Your sister, Shirley, told me you hate this grandmother.'

'That big mouth . . .' Tori is back to being foolish again. 'You can beat me up, or break my bones. I can't tell you what I don't know.'

'Now, sugar plum, I don't need to hurt your

sweet little bod. Your mama in prison is only a text message away from any guard in there. I give orders and,' he makes a throat-slashing gesture, 'bye-bye Mama.'

Tori leaps up and tries to jump on him, screaming, fists thrusting hopelessly. Dix grabs her easily. It amuses him.

I have to do something to stop this. 'Excuse me! Excuse me,' I say in a most pitiable way. 'Is it possible to take me to the nearest bathroom? It *has* been a number of hours since you brought us here and the bladder . . .' I shrug, helplessly.

Dix pushes Tori away. He is annoyed. He indicates one of the men. 'Hicks, take the old broad inside. But secure her first.'

Tori hides a smile and I make a show of creaking my 'old body' up off of the sleeping bag. The guy to whom I've been appointed rushes over to help the doddering old lady. Good, this one's the weakest in the link. Hickory, Dickory, Doc. The names start clicking in. Hicks, Dix. The other one, something like Docks. I remember.

Hicks gently applies the blindfold and duct tape, takes my arm and walks me out the back door.

Yes, it's definitely a garage. The smell of gasoline is even worse now. I peek through the bottom of the loosely tied blindfold and notice the SUV is gone and another car is in its place. Some old-fashioned looking car. Not good news. Jack and Morrie will be looking for an SUV.

Outside, I take a deep breath. The air feels so

217

good after the stuffiness of the shed. I was right. There *is* a garden of flower pots, and now I recognize the plant and its odor. It's lavender that I smell. Sweet, beautiful lavender. I'm getting excited. I know I've been here. Bless Izzy's heart. Lavender planted among the yucca. I peek under my blindfold. Garage with attached metal shed. Garden at the back of the house. Can it be? Omigod . . .! In the house, I'm brought to a bathroom. The nice guy, Hicks, takes my blindfold off, but just so I can see my way around in the bathroom. I have been in this bathroom.

And I now definitely know where I am. How is this possible? We are in Izzy's house. And of course Izzy isn't home. I know where he is. And then I recall, my jailbird's full name is Isadore Dix. The gang leader must be his son. What was it? Chaz. Izzy mentioned his son, Chaz, when we looked at his photo on the piano. Does Chaz know his father is in jail only a few blocks away?

I search the room quickly for something I can use as a weapon, but they've cleared everything out except one towel. Damn. I wish I could smash the glass of the little medicine cabinet above the sink, for a shard or two. But nothing to do it with, and besides, where would I hide the glass?

'Are you ready to come out?' calls Hicks. I say yes, and he opens the door and he gently puts the blindfold on again. Oh, Jack, if I only had a way to reach you!

Part Eight
The Rescue

Thirty-Nine
Jack and Morrie on the Job

It's after midnight. Father and son are at Jack's dining-room table, surrounded by city maps and drinking coffee to stay awake. Not that the coffee is working; their eyes are bleary. Their bodies ache. But they continue on. The map has been circled to where Jack had pointed out to Morrie the house the Woodleys once lived in.

'Let's sum up what we know,' Morrie suggests.

'Good idea,' says exhausted Jack.

Morrie says, 'Okay, we know about the original case in California. This was the fifteen-years-ago bank heist pulled by Fred and Helen Steiner. Police records showed that they'd arrested Helen – nine months pregnant. Fred was presumed dead. Witnesses in the bank attested that there were three others in on the robbery; none of the other three were caught and Helen Steiner refused to name names.'

Jack comments, 'They had undoubtedly threatened her to keep quiet; they'd take it out on her children and grandchildren. She knew how dangerous Dix was.'

Morrie adds, 'We learned from the La Mesa police that a cleaning woman at a local motel found three guys tied up in ropes, their mouths covered by duct tape. Then, feeling sorry for

221

them, thinking they were staying at the motel and had been robbed, she released them. To her surprise, they ran from the room and disappeared. Too bad the woman hadn't called the police while they were still trussed up. When the police were finally summoned by the manager, he and the police questioned all residents and no one owned the SUV with the slashed tires. The three men had been found in a room registered to Gloria Steiner. These men were not registered at the motel.'

Morrie continues. 'Too bad the police didn't break into the car at that time. We'd have their identities. They sent a truck to tow it, but by that time the SUV was also gone.'

Jack reads his notes from his conversation with Tori's two older sisters in LA.

'I guess I can say this older one is the brighter sister. The first one, Shirley, just kept moaning and hiccupping.

'Sister Marilyn told me an interesting story – that they had visited Tori's mother in prison and that's when Helen told Tori her father was still alive and she should go and find him. Mom slipped that photo of the Woodleys to her then and there.

'Remembering that Tori early on had playfully mentioned meeting three guys in La Mesa who drove a black SUV. Funny names for their tats – Hickory, Dickory and Docks. She joked about the "Dickory" as Dix. An unusual name. So, thinking that these might be the guys from LA, I asked Marilyn if she knew anyone with the name Dix, and Marilyn was surprised. There's a Charles Dix who is one of her mother's guards. Marilyn was shocked when I told her that a man named Dix came after Tori, believing the story and demanding that she reveal where her father is. Marilyn thinks about it and remembers that Dix was standing at the prison exit and must have heard Tori telling her sister about her father still being alive. But why would he have anything to do with Tori and her father?'

'You told her, Tori's been kidnapped?' Jack asks.

'It terrified her. She couldn't understand why any of this was happening. Marilyn continued to insist the story wasn't true. She was sure that her mother was mentally ill and this was all a fantasy. Their father was dead and buried; she had been to his funeral. To calm her, I promised her sister we'd call when Tori was found.'

Jack surmises, 'Could it be the same Dix, the prison guard, and his two pals in La Mesa? Can we assume they are the three other unnamed bank robbers?'

Morrie's eyes light up. 'I would. And we just arrested our coffee shop thief, Isadore Dix. A coincidence?'

Jack smiles. 'And we don't believe in coincidences.'

Morrie is on his laptop immediately. Jack watches his fingers fly across the letters. Morrie grins. 'No coincidence. Charles Dix, born 1972 in Davie, Florida. Father Isadore Dix, mother Eleanor Dix, deceased. How about that? Lived practically right next door to us.'

Jack whistles. 'Well, wadda ya know.'

Morrie says, 'We know a lot. We have a match. We're getting close.

Jack says, 'Tori couldn't have tackled those men alone. Must have been helped by the young men in the bus she mentioned.'

'Gutsy girl, Miss Tori. We now can assume she came here to find the Woodleys, who she was sure could lead her to her father. And those men want Daddy as well.'

'Well, the time has come. I think a visit to Isadore aka Izzy is in order. Dear old dad might aid us in finding his son.' He yawns. '*Mañana.*'

Jack walks him to the door. Morrie suggests his dad get some sleep.

As if he could rest until he found his Gladdy.

Forty
Bedtime Stories

Midnight in the shed. The heat beat heavily down on us during the day, but now the metal has cooled down and Tori is shivering. The shed is creepy without any light; yet it isn't totally black and there is some ambient light from cracks in the metal ceiling. Enough so we can see one another, but barely.

Most of the tacos that was purported to be our dinner are half-eaten. Cold and tasteless, they lie in their original wrapping from some nearby Mexican take-out, along with the water bottles we consumed. Our captors gave us a last bathroom break along with a threat that we'd better come up with answers in the morning, and now we are attempting to sleep.

I told Tori earlier that I knew where we were; that we are hidden at the home of Dix's father. This is good news. She jumps up, excited. 'Then his dad will call the cops.'

I had to let her down. 'His dad is in jail.' I didn't bother to tell her, I helped put him there.

'Dead end,' she said, unhappily.

'But it means we're close by. It gives me hope.'

She doesn't bother to answer.

Hicks, bless his heart, is our only helper. He is clearly not happy with being a kidnapper. At 'dinnertime' he slipped me his tiny pocket keychain flashlight and I am grateful.

I am tired enough to sleep. I used to pride myself on being able to sleep anywhere, anytime, but how can I with Tori thrashing around in her sleeping bag?

I sit up.

'Wanna play a game?'

Tori pulls herself up, and stares at me as if I were something demented.

'Let's pretend we are camping out.'

Cranky Tori sneers. 'You gotta be kidding.'

'Humor me. You have something better to do? Have a late date with someone? The cute one in New Mexico?'

She manages to crack a smile. 'I wish. Okay, cray lady, I'll play along.'

'We are on a beautiful finely grained sandy beach on our own private island and we have a bonfire blazing. Can you hear mandolins playing in the background?'

'Yeah sure. Mandolins on a private island.' Tori twists her body into a more comfortable position, still looking at me as if I'd just escaped the looney bin.

I wave Hick's tiny flashlight beam up onto her face. 'See the flames?'

'Anyone ever tell you, you're nutso?'

'No. Not lately. Okay, ready for our marshmallows?'

'Whatever, weird lady.'

I hand the flashlight over to Tori. I pretend I am holding a stick and I place an imaginary marshmallow on the imaginary stick, making sure it will stay on. 'How burnt do you like yours?'

I get a silly grin. 'Totally burned. Until the outside is black and the inside mush.'

'Got it.' I pretend to cook 'it' over the 'fire', then hand her the imaginary stick. Tori takes it and pretends along with me. Soon she is 'eating' her marshmallow and seems like she's enjoying it.

'Yum,' she says. 'Delicious, now what?' Her tone is still one of humoring me.

'Now we talk. Game of Truth. What's on your mind, Tori who used to be Gloria, that stops you from falling asleep?'

For a moment, she glares at me, then she bursts into tears. 'It's none of your business!'

I say nothing and wait. I don't want to break up her speech. She is ready to blow.

'I hate my life! I hate everybody! I hate myself!

I look in a mirror every day and I wish I was anyone else but me.'

'Why?'

'I'm ashamed of how I treat my grandma. I hate that I made her cry. But I hate that she abandoned us and left me with a mother she helped put in prison and being raised by two mean other grandparents. She robbed me of a happy childhood.'

'You have a right to be angry.'

Tori stares at me, surprised. I'm sure she expected me not to take her side. 'Your turn. What kind of childhood did *you* have?'

I think of what to say. 'I had immigrant parents, and they only spoke Polish, and kids in school made fun of me because I spoke very little English and had a funny accent.'

'What did you do? Did you beat them up?'

I laugh. 'Not my generation. I just ignored them and they stopped. I worked very hard on learning how to sound like everyone else and also to avoid toxic kids. But I was angry at my parents. I wanted an "American mom and dad", like the others had. Years later I understood how it had been for them. Think about it – forced to leave your home that you love, for fear of being killed. Imagine how frightening it had to be, traveling thousands of miles away, to a strange land where you don't know the language, with little or no money, not knowing what lies ahead. Later, I finally grew up and realized how brave they were.'

'Grandma and Grandpa Steiner spoke with thick German accents.'

'Did you ever ask them about their childhood and how they came to this country?'

'No, never. I only thought about myself.' She lowers her head, feeling guilty.

'It sounds like they were disappointed. Maybe they had a fantasy about how wonderful things would be in the new country. Maybe they were unhappy in themselves or the life they led.'

'And maybe they were unhappy that they were stuck with a brat like me.'

'Could be. Really a mean and rotten brat like you?' I'm teasing her.

Tori nods, grins. 'The worst.' And I smile with her. 'I never thought about it. Grandma Ida had gone, Mom in prison, Dad thought to be dead. My sisters were much older and had no patience for me. I guess there was no one to turn to.'

'The Steiners might have said no – but they didn't. They willingly agreed to raise you.'

She's giggling now. 'And boy, were they sorry.'

'They probably did the best they could.'

'I suppose . . . but they could have tried harder. And I could have tried to understand.'

'They had an only son who robbed a bank and had run away and was thought to be dead. That had to be hard on them.'

Some silence, then, Tori stretches. 'I think I can sleep now.' She frowns. 'But I can't. I always go to bed with a book and read till my eyes close. No book here.' She lies down again, and twists and turns.

A few moments of silence, 'Well, maybe not a juicy novel. But you still have Hy's Hialeah

228

racetrack program. You can try to count horses instead of sheep.'

We both laugh again, remembering what I said to Dix.

Tori lies down and browses the program using the flashlight. Her eyes close very soon and I'm pleased to see the child now smiling in her sleep. I reach over and retrieve the flashlight and the program.

Now I am wide awake again. Maybe it will work for me as well. Ha ha. I lean against a wall and open the program and immediately think of my dad. I will try to guess who he might have bet on, had he been there. So many fond memories. Dad always included me on his racetrack days. Even let me try to pick the winners. He and his friends used to get a kick out of the choices I made. I picked horses with the cutest names. All losers. They teased me, but they were kind and put up with me. The years I spent leaning against that rail with him and his cronies will come in useful right now. He taught me well and I know how to handicap. I'll start with first race. See if I'd have picked the ones who won.

A few minutes later, my eyes prop wide open. 'Omigod!' I say. 'Omigod!'

I didn't sleep the rest of the night.

Forty-One
Another Sleepless Night

The three guys slump at Izzy's kitchen table. The bones and fatty remains of a roasted chicken lie there, along with leftover greasy French fries and six empty beer bottles and an equally empty bottle of cheap scotch. They are tired, grumpy and drunk. And they are quarrelling. Well, two at least, Dix and Hicks. Dockson is lying with his head on the table, snoring. What's left of his food is next to his nose. Neither of the two is aware, nor care, that the sky is lightening and clouds are soon to appear ringed with bright orange and red coloring, proclaiming another sweltering day in which to suffer.

Hicks is angry. 'The kid doesn't know anything. So what now?' Hicks pounds on the table. 'You're beating a dead horse.'

Dockson mumbles his annoyance.

Dix pounds back. 'I tell you, she does!'

'But if she doesn't? What then?'

Dix picks up his gun and twirls his finger around the trigger. 'I kill her, that's what.' He grins and it's an ugly sight.

Hicks is sweating by now. From fury, not enough sleep and too much booze. It's giving him the confidence he hasn't had before. 'Yeah, you are so easy with that gun. You're so quick

230

wanting to kill. If it wasn't for poor Helen taking the rap, you'd be on the other side of that cell door with her. You beat up that woman year after year and she never gave you up.'

'I told you never to mention that again!' His eyes seem blood-red and livid.

'Now you reward her by wanting to kill her kid!'

'Since when do you care about dear Tori?'

'Since this useless trip started. She's a kid with a fairy-tale daddy who doesn't exist. She needed an excuse to run away and that was it.' He spits. 'We should have quit on the road. Now look at the mess you put us in. Kidnapping is a federal offense with life in prison. That's what we'll get out of this!'

Hicks gets up and paces, zigzagging up and down the room. 'This whole trip is a disaster. Stupid idea coming all this way for nothing. Even if Fred was still around, which I doubt, after fifteen years that money would be gone! I don't know why I let you talk me into this stupidity.'

'Even if he spent every dime of that two hundred thousand, I want at him! I want him twisting in the wind. I'm gonna kill the bastard for cheating me!'

'Cheating *you*? It's always been all about you!'

'You want out, then get the hell out right now.' Dix stops fiddling with the gun and points it at Hicks.

'Yeah, right, I start for the door and you shoot me in the back. What'll you do with my body?'

'I remember a nice garden outside.'

Nothing to lose anymore, he cries out, 'Dumb

ass, your daddy's flowers are in pots, there is no garden.' Dix glares at him. 'If it wasn't for you and that damn gun, we wouldn't be here today.'

Dix glares back. 'What the hell are you jabbering about?'

'It would all been so easy if you hadn't shot off your mouth along with your gun. It got everyone in the bank panicking. We would have been in and out, and home free, but no, you had to show off! You had to let the scared crowd know you were the boss!'

Dix drops the gun on the table and leaps up. 'You've been bitching all through this trip, so beat it. You either do it my way . . . or head for the highway.'

Like two enraged bulls they face off at one another, snarling.

Hicks manages a wry smile. 'I can't. I have to protect that girl from you.'

'Is that so? Like hell you will.'

Dix, maddened, crazed, with fists clenched, rushes at Hicks, who is caught off guard. He falls down, pulling Dix down and onto him. They roll across the room, knocking into kitchen chairs and anything else in their way, punching at each other. Huffing and puffing and groaning.

Dockson, half awake complains, 'Go some-wheres else, I'm sleeping here!'

'Shut up!' Dix shouts up at him.

'All right,' Dockson says cheerfully, turning his face to his other side. The snoring follows immediately.

The two sweating pugilists get up and leave the room, going in opposite directions.

232

Forty-Two
Hy and Sophie Finally Remember

Jack heads for his old Mercedes, looking at his watch. Good. Nine a.m. He'll be on time to meet Morrie at the station. Today will be a big day, he hopes. Looks like another scorcher. He takes off his seersucker jacket and tosses it into the back seat, and rolls up his sleeves. He is about to get into the car when he hears, 'Wait! Wait for me! Don't go!'

Jack sees Hy, waving something in his hand, coming at him at as furious a pace as his roly-poly body can manage.

'What's up?'

Hy reaches Jack, out of breath. 'My memory came back. I knew it would. You know how it is. Ya have the words on the tip of your tongue. Then you have to wait till your memory sizzles through the whole brain until it finds it again. I usually get stuff back in a few minutes, but this took longer—'

Jack interrupts. 'I have an appointment . . .'

'Oh, sorry. But this is red-hot information.' He pushes the Hialeah program at him. 'I save them all. Good thing I do. Look at the first race.'

233

Jack peers at the page, not getting it, keeps scanning. Hy can't stand it; Jack's too slow. He pokes at the words, and keeps poking. 'Look at the names! Look!'

A moment later, 'Omigod!'

Hy beams. 'You might say I've solved your case.'

Jack says, 'Get in the car! I'm taking you with me to Morrie.'

Hy eagerly jumps into the passenger seat, straps himself in and Jack starts the motor. Lola watches her darling leaving. She waves. Hy waves back. Her hero!

As Jack is about to turn left from Building P, he hears:

'Yoo hoo, don't go! Wait for us!'

Both men look out the window to see Sophie and Bella hurrying as fast as their arthritic legs allow. 'We need to tell you something important,' says Sophie. 'It's about Izzy's house! We finally remembered.' They reach the car, breathing hard.

Jack says, 'All right, get in. I'm late. We'll talk at the precinct.'

Eagerly they lift themselves into the back, Sophie carefully folding Jack's jacket out of her way. Hy is as surprised to see them as they are to see him.

All the way to the police station:

Sophie. 'Oy, remembering your memories is such a mish-mash.'

Hy. 'Yeah. Right.'

Sophie. 'You try to remember and you try and nothing comes when you want it.'

Hy, with a world-weary sigh. 'It's always on the tip of the tongue.'

Bella says nothing. She just moans.

Hy continues to lecture on what he considers his fine knowledge on the subject of memory, as Sophie nods along with him, and Bella remains unhappy.

Jack tunes them out as he drives. His mind is rattling with the amazing new information he now has. Thanks to, of all people, Hy Binder.

Meeting is called to order in Morrie's office. Hy and the women all want to talk at once. Morrie calms them down with coffee and some stale cookies that his assistant manages to dredge up. He couldn't find decaf for the ladies, but they settle for tea.

Hy and Jack get him to look at the racing program. 'Amazing,' he says.

Jack agrees. 'Right under our noses. Panorama Stables, purposely named after the city Tori lived in. The elusive horse breeders and owners, Harvey and Lila Woodley – now found at last. And their business partner, Mr Frank Sterner (not far off from Fred Steiner; why do people in hiding tend to use their real first initials?). Tori was right. Tori's daddy is alive.'

'What about us?' Sophie asks. 'We know something just as important.'

Hy razzes them. 'Not as big as mine.'

'Speak up, ladies,' Morrie invites.

Sophie takes another sip of her tea, pats her lips with a tissue and is finally ready to perform. Bella sighs.

'Well, it's like this. We went to Izzy's house

235

to feed his fish and water his plants. Being in jail prevents him doing it himself.'

Jack tries to nudge her into getting to her point. 'Perfectly sensible. Do go on.'

'Well, we get the key from under the rock like Izzy told us . . .'

'Move it along, babe,' insists Hy, that man of little patience. He's annoyed that his fifteen minutes of fame has been overshadowed by those two irritating women.

Bella tries to get in a word. 'Jackie, you did say even if something is silly . . .'

'I'm talking here, Bella.' Sophie interrupts 'Anyway, I'm downstairs giving the little fishies their lunch when Bella decides to go upstairs and snoop.'

'It's not snooping. I like looking at furnishings.'

'Whatever you want to call it. I say, snooping. Then she comes racing downstairs to tell me,' she pauses for dramatic effect, 'she saw a ghost.'

'I did.'

'You did not, there are no such things as ghosts.' Sophie now turns lawyer-inquisitor. 'Where were you, when you saw the alleged ghost?'

Hy can't resist. 'That babe watches too much *Law and Order*.'

Sophie ignores him. Jack and Morrie are being patient, as well as amused. They doubt this will take them anywhere. Sophie waits for Bella's answer, tapping her nails on Morrie's desk.

'I thought I heard water running so I went to the upstairs bathroom and there he was. The room was filled with clouds of air.'

Sophie interrupts, taps her foot impatiently.

236

'Not clouds. It must have been steam from hot water. Describe what your "ghost" was wearing?'

'It was kind of a white flowing thing.' Bella frowns; it feels like her best friend is betraying her.

Even Jack can't resist. 'A Greek toga?'

'Yes, a toga.'

Sophie huffs. 'Let me translate. There's a naked man wearing a towel who just got out of the tub. Now who on earth would be taking a shower in Izzy's house?'

Jack and Morrie, finally getting it, practically jump out of their seats. 'Izzy's son?' Jack says.

Morrie adds, 'Charles "Chaz" Dix! Of course, his father's house, the perfect place to hide. Bella's ghost!'

Jack. 'Incredible. Let's get going.' They are already moving their guests toward the door.

Sophie is confused. 'I was thinking, it was someone homeless, who needed a shower.'

The two men are galvanized into action; Morrie, says, 'Before we jump the gun, let's get Izzy down here. Now.'

Morrie turns to the three helpers, who are beaming now. 'You've all done something very important, now us cop guys need to take over. I'll have one of my men take you home.

Jack shakes Hy's hand. 'You *are* a hero.'

Hy pretends humility, and fails at it.

Then Jack hugs both ladies. 'You, too.'

And they are ushered out. Grinning.

Jack and Morrie shake their heads. 'Utterly astonishing.' Morrie picks up his police radio.

Jack teases his son. 'Brilliant deductions, great police work, wouldn't you say?'

237

Forty-Three
Gladdy and Tori Get It

I can hardly wait for Tori to wake up. She needs her rest, but I must tell her. I shake her. 'Tori. Up. Up. Now!'

Still sleepy, she rubs her eyes.

'I have incredibly good news for you.' I hand her a last water bottle. 'Throw some water on your face.' I am clutching the racetrack program in my other hand.

Tori stretches. 'Is it morning? Is it even light out there?'

'I think so, I don't know, but pay attention.'

'I have to pee.'

'Don't think about it, look at this.' I pull her up into a sitting position.'

'What? Why?'

I hand her the program, that missive of great news. 'Look at the names of the horses that Hy won in the first race and the third when Hy picked a long shot owned by the same breeders. Read them out loud.'

Tori leans with her back to the wall, so she can get comfortable and read easily. 'Temple Star. Glory Girl. M&M.'

She looks at me, puzzled. So what?'

'Grandma Ida told me that your mom and dad loved going to the movies. They even used movie-star nicknames for themselves. Old time stars: Helen Hayes and Fred Astaire. Now tell me your name and your sisters' names.'

'I'm Tori,' she says, sarcastic again. 'Like as if you don't know?'

'No, your mother did not name you Tori.'

Slowly now, thinking; something is happening. 'Gloria. Marilyn. Shirley.'

'You might not know this old-timer. But the famous Gloria was Gloria Swanson.'

Starting to catch on. 'She used to call me Morning Glory.'

'Marilyn Monroe. Shirley Temple,' I add.

Tori reads from the program again. 'Temple Star. Glory Girl and M&M. Omigod! Omigod, they're clues, they're meant to be clues!'

'Now read the name of the owners and don't forget their partner.' I'm trying to keep calm, but Tori is kicking her legs in the air.

'Mr & Mrs Harvey Woodley at Panorama Stables! The Woodleys, at last! Panorama, named after the city where we lived!' She looks again. 'Their partner is Frank Sterner! He couldn't use his real name or the cops would find him. Same first initials. It's my dad! We found him. You found him! Tori looks up at me in amazement.

Her face brightens. 'Mama tried to tell me. Where the flamingos fly. They live at the racetrack. Omigod!'

'That's what I said.'

'He's been sending all those clues for me to find him!'

'Probably.'

She jumps up and grabs my arms and swings me around. 'He's alive. He's really alive. I looked so long and there they were, so close by.'

She's laughing, then crying, but still dancing. I am just about to warn her that we need to keep this quiet.

Too late. We hear the applause. We freeze. Dix and his sidekicks are standing inside the shed, staring at us from the back door, hands clapping.

'How nice to see such happy faces,' Dix says, nastily. 'Now why would that be?'

Tori drops back down on her sleeping bag, hiding the racing program behind her. With a quick look back as she does so.

I know what's coming and there's nothing I can do about it.

Dix moves in close to her. I can see Hicks frowning and Dockson looking clueless, as usual.

'Ever play poker, Tori?' He smiles, but it's an unpleasant grimace.

She shakes her head, scared now.

'A good gambler watches the other players and looks for the "tell". Know what a tell is?'

Tori shakes her head again.

'When a player gets a really exciting card or hand, he can't resist one teeny, tiny look. It's a giveaway. He looks and then I know what he's got, and then I know I've got him beat.'

All is silent. Tori is miserable.

'You looked back. That was your tell. Hand it over, cutie pie.'

She hangs her head down, refusing to look at him.

'Don't be stupid. Do it the easy way or we do it my way.'

Tori stares up at me. I close my eyes; we are helpless.

'No!' Tori won't give up.

Poor, sweet heroic girl, I think.

'It's nothing, nothing that would interest you!' She practically throws her body over the program.

Dix grins. 'Let me be the judge of that.'

'I knew you were holding out on me,' he says purposefully, looking at Hicks, saying it to prove his point, Hicks turns away, unhappily.

Dix then shrugs, nods to Dockson. Dockson marches over to Tori, pushes her down, then turns her over. She struggles to keep it away from him, but he's way too strong and he grabs the program in seconds and knocks her back down again.

Dockson hands it to Dix.

'I need to go to the bathroom,' she shrieks.

'You get to go when I know what made you so happy.'

I walk over to him; I am quivering with rage. 'Enough, big shot, let her go inside and I'll tell you what you want to know.'

Dix looks at me in a way that curdles the blood. Suddenly, weepy Grandma turns tough? He's impressed. He nods to Dockson.

Dockson puts on the blindfold and takes Tori out, kicking and yelling. He's slapping the duct tape over her mouth as they go.

I notice that Hicks has been left out of this. He stands there, board-stiff. Trouble in Paradise?

Dix doesn't need my help, he sees the names

immediately, and gets it. Dix is not only cruel, but he is also smart. He waves the program at Hicks. 'You were worried about money. Looks like Daddy struck it rich. Not only is he alive, but he's loaded!'

'You got what you want. Let us out,' I say.

'Nice try, Grandma, but you'll stay right here. Maybe we'll come back for you, maybe not.' He pinches my cheek. If I were Tori, I'd spit in his face. But even though I want to, I'm not Tori. And I don't.

Dockson returns with Tori. Removes the blindfold and tape. She kicks him in the leg. He jumps around in pain. Dockson smacks her. Dix thinks it's funny.

The three men hurry to the door.

'Stay cool,' the bastard calls to us.

Then they are gone. We are bereft.

Tori comes to me and we hug. I want to say something hopeful, but why bother? I feel just as defeated as she does.

And the cruel, unfeeling sun is beginning to heat up the shed.

Forty-Four
Izzy Now on the Job

Izzy is jumping for joy. 'I knew somebody would bail me out. Who's the Good Samaritan?' He is wearing his old suit again. Gone is his jail garb.

242

Jack and Morrie eye the performance with jaded indifference.

Morrie says, 'Not quite what you think. We're borrowing you for a short while.'

Jack jumps in. 'You're going to play a part to help us on a sting.'

His eyes light up. 'I know what that means. I saw the movie. Robert Redford. Paul Newman. Who do I get to play?' Izzy is still high on this unexpected respite from his jail cell.

Morrie continues. 'I have some interesting news for you. You have a house guest.'

Izzy's eyebrows cross and meet in center confusion. 'What? Who? Where? At my house four blocks away?'

'That's the one. We believe he is staying there with two friends.'

'Is he, whoever he is, the one bailing me out?'

Morrie shrugs. 'There is no bailing out here. We want to take you to your house; we want you to get your key from under the rock—'

Izzy interrupts. 'How do you know about my hiding place? It's a secret.'

Jack snorts. 'Every one in the world hides their key under a rock. Couldn't you have come up with something more original?'

Morrie says, 'Congratulations, your son Charles is staying in your house.'

Izzy is dazed. 'What? My boy, Chaz?'

Morrie speaks quickly. 'Listen, time is important here. We'll fill you in as we go, but we need to leave right now.'

'Okay, that's very nice of you to let me have this visit . . .'

Morrie stops him. 'No, this is not pleasure, this is business. We need you to play a part. In this sting.'

'I always liked Paul Newman in that movie.'

'Okay, our star, Isadore Dix, is playing Paul Newman. You will be coming home and using your key to get in, and act surprised. Your son is there and you will be thrilled to see him. You will keep him busy. We'll take it from there.'

'I *will* be surprised and thrilled. I haven't seen my boy in about thirty years, but why now? And take what from where? What's going on? I heard that people charge big money for using their houses. In stings. And movies, too.'

Morrie ignores him so Jack answers. 'That's in Hollywood. Making movies. Not here. Sorry.'

A policeman sticks his head through the door. 'Everyone is in place. We've got them surrounded.'

Morrie starts for the door. 'Let's hit the road.'

As Izzy is led to the door; he asks, 'Is there some payment for this role? What about residuals? A SAG card? What's in it for me?'

Forty-Five
Those Darn Church Bells

Jack is nervous. Everything depends on Dix and his guys being surprised.

Izzy does as he was told. However, in his premier role of actor, he makes a big production of picking up his key and unlocking the door.

He can't resist the joke. He calls out, about to cross the threshold, 'Honey, I'm home,' then turns and winks at Morrie, who glares back at him. Morrie makes arm-shuffling gestures and Izzy whispers, 'Okay, I'm going. I'm going!' He enters, shutting the door behind him.

'How long do we wait?' Jack asks from their hiding place in the bushes.

'Give him ten minutes.'

One of his police cadre comes from behind the house. 'The car is gone,' he reports.

They had sent a chopper up earlier and it was reported that some older version of a Ford sedan was seen in the open garage.

Morrie is disturbed. 'Not good.' And no sign of the black SUV anywhere in the neighborhood.

Just then, Izzy pokes his head out. He shrugs. 'Nobody home.'

'Damn it, we're too late!' He brings his men in from around the perimeter and orders them to search every inch of the house. 'Find Gladdy and Tori! They must be here somewhere!'

Jack is worried. 'Maybe they've taken them along with them to a different hiding place. Is it possible they knew we were coming?'

Morrie swears. 'Unlikely. All bases are covered! They have to be here.'

Izzy whines. 'My first chance to see my boy and I missed him.'

The policemen are back downstairs in record time. They've looked everywhere. The house is empty. They found suitcases. And scraps of food on the kitchen table, razors and toiletry in bathrooms, but nothing else.

Suddenly there is an ear-piercing sound; church bells ringing so close, you would think you were directly in their bell tower. Hands clasp ears. The sound is deafening.

'What the hell?' This from Jack.

Izzy shouts proudly, 'That's our local church around the corner. Telling us it's Sunday, twelve noon.'

Morrie shouts back, 'This is crazy. I can't hear you. Let's get out of here. Now!'

In the shed, Gladdy and Tori have covered their ears as well.

Tori is in a panic. She yells, 'I swear I heard voices out there!'

'The guys are back again?' I practically shriek to be heard.

'No, it's many different voices. I could hear them in the garage.'

Young ears, our Tori has. I didn't hear anything.

'We've got to signal them.' Tori pulls off her boots and races around the shed, banging the heels from wall to wall. She's already soaked in sweat, from the heat that's radiating, and slowly suffocating us.

'Gladdy, help me!'

I can barely pull off my shoes. I'm already weakened from the heat. I can hardly move. What little water we had, I wasted, throwing it in Tori's face to wake her. 'Tori, it's useless with those damn bells!'

She can't hear me anyway; she continues to pound.

With every ounce of strength I can manage, I am pounding, too.

The bells finally stop ringing. The cops are taking off. Morrie and Jack stand there, shaking their heads, as if to remove the noise still in their ears.

Izzy grins. 'Every Sunday, like clockwork.' He enjoys his pun. 'Wakes up the whole neighborhood. Church-goers have no excuse to sleep in. Like they didn't hear their alarm clocks?'

Morrie starts hurrying down the driveway, and looks back. Jack hasn't moved. 'What? What are you waiting for?'

'I think I hear something.' He bends, as if to listen.

'Yeah, we'll be hearing that ringing in our ears all day.' Morrie starts to move again.

'Listen.'

Izzy adds. 'I hear it, too. A different kind of noise.'

Jack is like someone possessed. He is following

247

the sound. Around the side of the house, past the potted plants, moving toward the open garage.

In moments, Morrie and Izzy catch up.

All three stop in their tracks. Listening. Realizing that there is a hammering of metal and it's coming from inside the shed!

Jack starts hitting his fists onto the shed. Shouting, 'Gladdy! Gladdy?'

The pounding stops and he can hear both our voices.

'Jack!' I can hardly speak.

'Get us out of here!' Tori shouts.

Morrie is furious with himself. 'I thought they searched here! Dammit!'

Jack shouts, moving around the metal shack, 'How do we get into this damn thing?'

Izzy yells. 'There's a door back inside! Follow me!' Morrie and Jack race Izzy into the empty garage.

Jack hits at the complicated lock connecting metal door. In seconds, Tori calls out. 'Duh! It's locked! If it wasn't, we'd be out where you are. I hope you have some muscle to get us out! And you better hurry before we drop dead!'

Jack calls back. 'Hold on, Tori. Just hold on.'

'Yeah, easy for you say. We're in a sauna, here. Ever hear of a sauna without a towel? Try to move a little faster, big guy.'

'Kid's got a mouth on her.' Morrie examines the lock carefully.

'She sure does.' Jack says it proudly.

Morrie looks to Izzy. 'Keys?'

Izzy shakes his head, pointing up to an empty wall key-holder. 'They're gone.'

248

I cry out again, but I am so weak; I worry that he won't be able to hear me.

'Hurry, darling, we can't breathe.'

Jack kicks at the door, desperate.

'Wait,' Izzy says, 'I got tools.'

Jack and Morrie run after him to the other side of his potted plants. Jack sees a shovel, grabs it.

Jack is sweating. Desperate. Tries as hard as he can to break the lock with the shovel. It isn't working. He is near tears of frustration.

Tori's voice again, snippy. 'Where's Spiderman when we need him?'

Morrie yells to us to get away from the inside of the door. He pushes Jack aside, points his weapon, takes aim and shoots at the lock. It shatters bits of metal, but the lock remains unaffected.

Izzy apologizes. 'I spent a lot of money on that lock. It's extra strong.'

Morrie asks, 'You keep something important in that shed?'

'No, it's empty.'

Jack, still pounding the shovel at the unbreakable device, glares at him. 'You have an expensive car you keep in this open garage, and you lock an empty shed?'

Izzy shrugs. He never thought of that.

Tori continues to shout from inside. 'What's taking you dorks so long? I'll be late for my Hatha Yoga class!' More banging on the metal.

They no longer hear my voice and I'm sure Jack is frightened.

Morrie calls on his phone for special assistance. Morrie and Izzy stand back to wait, helpless,

except for Jack who keeps banging away hopelessly with the shovel.

One of Morrie's men has returned. A cop is now
running up the driveway, carrying an electric
saw. Morrie practically has to drag Jack out of
the way of the door. He doesn't want to stop
trying.

Morrie, to the cop, 'You know what to do?'

'Yes, sir.' Within minutes he works the saw in a
circle around the metal surrounding the lock. Once
the hole is made, the lock drops to the ground.

Tori grins through the hole. 'Mr Cop, make it
a little larger, okay?'

Jack pulls his way into the now easily opened
shed, leaping over the broken lock, shouting for
me. Tori, holding her boots, is already rushing
out the open door, gives him a quick kiss as they
pass one another. 'Wifey said you'd come.
You're fab! If I didn't have a father, I'd want
you to be him!' She yells, 'Water, water all
around, and not a drop to drink!'

Jack finds me leaning against a wall, my hands
trying to protect my face from the burning heat.
I am barely breathing. I can't even imagine the
temperature inside. Jack gently half walks, half
carries me.

Outside, Tori is gulping water from the nearest
hose brought to her by Izzy. Between swallows
she shouts, 'Don't just stand there. They're on
their way to the racetrack. My dad is there! My
dad is alive!'

Jack says to us, 'We know, we figured it out,
too.'

250

Tori hugs them. Morrie. The cop with the saw, and even Izzy.

With that, the group is running down the driveway, jumping into cars.

Morrie shouts. 'Jack. Gladdy. Get down here.'

Tori can't resist the last word. 'Yeah, and they've got guns. Let's move it!'

After I gulp eagerly at the water in the hose, Jack and I hug tightly. It was a close call and we know it. 'If I lost you . . .'

'But you didn't, my darling.'

Forty-Six
The Racetrack

Jack wants to send me home. I insist on going with him. 'You need to rest,' he argues.

'Later. I can help right now. I know what those guys look like.' I insist on riding to the racetrack with them, and so I do. I'm not going to let them talk me out of it. Tori is going to find her father, I know she will, and I want to be there to witness it.

On our arrival, we are quickly given heads-ups from Morrie's cops already on site: They report that the Woodleys are no longer in their Panorama Stables area. Neither are they at the paddocks, where horses were saddled before each race. Two of their horses are running today. They've been told they are seated somewhere in the grandstand where they always watch the races. But no one could tell them exactly where they sit.

Tori dashes off on her own. Jack and Morrie join his men searching the park for Dix and his partners, equipped with only a blurred photo of the prison guard. Izzy, unrealistic, yet hopeful, and totally excited, insists he would be useful even though he hasn't seen his son since he ran away in his teen years. 'A father would know his son, no matter what,' says Izzy, who would say anything not to be in his jail cell. But would a daughter recognize a father she never met?

I fear my Jack and Morrie are working against poor odds. This place is enormous. And a race-track win is all about having the best odds.

They won't let me go with them. I assume they think I would only be in the way. Jack insists I stay safe. He wants me to rest. Over and over, I insist I am fine. So, here I am where he planted me, high above in the clubhouse area. With a pair of binoculars offered by one of Morrie's cops, along with a cell phone in case I need anything. Giving me a made-up title of 'Spotter'. Assume I'm far away from danger. Leaving me frustrated and useless.

So, as I sit off and out of the action, I reminisce about what I know of Hialeah from years ago when I often spent days at the track with my dad. The smells are still the same. Horsey odors; hay vying with food smells; hot dogs, cotton candy. Hialeah stretches over two hundred acres, with stunning buildings and gorgeous gardens, and a huge lake; once considered one of the most beautiful parks in the country.

But times have changed, and not for the better. There are no longer thoroughbred races. The greats – like Seabiscuit, War Admiral and Citation – raced here with cheering crowds numbering in the thousands. Jockeys like Arcaro and Shoemaker rode the biggest and best. The gorgeous flamingos are still here, living in the infield perched among the gardens and lake, their breeds' home for more than a century.

There is only quarter horse racing these days, and even though there are no longer the huge crowds, Morrie and men will still have trouble finding Dix in this huge stadium. I can spot his men circling, going up and down the steps, searching for three guys who look dangerous.

The bugler in his red 'hunting' uniform comes out in front of the stands and blows the call to the post for the fifth race. A sight and sound that has always thrilled me. It still thrills me. For a moment, I'm a teenager, back with my father, the two of us hanging on the rail, in anticipation, waving our arms, screaming, cheering our chosen horse in. My dad, a genius at picking winners, even though I didn't realize his were only two-dollar bets; we didn't have enough money to waste. As a small child, that's how I saw him. A winner, bringing home his small profit.

I raise my binocs to watch the next batch of horses trot toward the starting gate across from the infield. They pass the stands and around the clubhouse and enter the area where they will wait.

It takes a while to get all the horses in their stalls. Then the starter's button sounds and – they're off!

Then I remember why I'm here.

Where is Jack and Morrie and Morrie's men right now?

Where are the Woodleys?

Where is Tori?

But worse, where are the evil men who intend to murder? Especially Dix, the most dangerous of the three?

With my binocs I excitedly find Tori and I track her as she searches the stands, aisle by aisle, and I have to smile. After all Ida and I went through to finagle her to buy 'acceptable' clothes to go to the track, she's in her old jeans, dirty tee, and boots, even grungier due to the time spent sweating, bath-less, in Izzy's shed.

If I had a racing form, or a program, I'd know which race will feature a Panorama Stables entry. I could ask someone to let me borrow their program, but no one is seated close enough to ask. And I must keep searching. The fifth race has just ended, but the Woodleys either didn't have a horse running in that one, or lost. This happy owner, and his trainer, who are now being photographed in the Winner's Circle with his winning horse and jockey, is definitely someone else.

For a moment, Tori can hardly move. She stands in front of the private box where three people sit. They have been in her dreams so long and now she can only gaze upon them in awe. Such an amazing journey, over at last.

She sees the puzzlement in the threesome facing this unknown, rather grubby-looking girl, who seems about to enter and intrude upon their privacy. The couple leaning close to one another is how she always imagined the Woodleys would look. Smart, beautiful, sophisticated, richly clothed and self-assured. And next to them; of course, her father! Her beautiful, definitely alive, long-lost father!

Tori can hardly breathe. She stares at him, drinking in his handsomeness. She can see how much she resembles him. Same curly hair, same light brown color, though his has beginning streaks of gray.

But when she looks into those hazel eyes exactly like hers, Tori can recognize the pain. She has seen that same pain when she glances at herself in a mirror. She wouldn't be able to name it but she senses that it is the pain of loss. Of being taken from her mother at birth, of losing her grandmother, Ida. A father she never knew.

Tori, probably for the first time in her life, is speechless.

Below and in front of them, other horses will race, horses will win and horses will lose, and handicappers will choose their next bets, and the crowd will shout and wave their arms, but for this group of four, time stands still.

Lila Woodley speaks, 'Can we help you, dear? Are you lost?'

Not anymore, she thinks. Tori smiles, with irony,

and finds herself recalling when Gladdy taught her how to correctly dress for the track, and how she would be laughing right now. Here Tori is, at the most important moment of her life, in dirty, smelly clothes, and desperately in need of a bath. She's a mess. She runs her fingers though her tangled hair. Oh, well, there's nothing she can do about it.

She takes a deep breath and fully enters the box and turns to Fred. She can barely get the word out. 'Daddy?'

Suddenly all three sit straighter, alert. Staring at this piteous creature.

'Gloria?' Fred's eyes light up, joyfully.

Tori nods, feeling the tears that begin falling down her cheeks.

'I can't believe you found me.'

She can't believe it either. She runs into his outstretched arms. He hugs her tightly. His streaming tears mingling with hers.

She doesn't know what to say, so she blurts out, 'Nobody calls me Gloria. I'm Tori. Please, I'm Tori.'

Fred grins. 'Tori, that's a nice name. Let's go with that.'

More hugging, with the Woodleys watching; they're also in tears.

'You've grown up so beautiful,' Fred says to his daughter.

Tori says to her father, 'And you're really real. Sometimes I doubted it; it seemed so crazy that you were alive. But, I just knew Mom was telling the truth. I wanted, so badly, for Mom to be telling the truth. I wanted to find my daddy.'

'She has your eyes,' Mrs Woodley says softly.

'And your curly hair,' adds Mr Woodley, grinning.

'What's left of it,' Fred laughs.

They beckon Tori to sit down. She does, but doesn't let go of her father's hand; as if it were a dream, she didn't want it to end. 'I'm sorry I'm dressed so badly . . . It's a long story.'

'You look beautiful to me,' says her smiling father.

'How did you know us?' Harvey Woodley says, wiping the tears from his eyes.

Tori pulls the well-worn photo out of her pocket and holds it out to them. 'I recognized you all from your photo.'

Lila Woodley glances at it and laughs. 'From a thirty-year-old black-and-white snapshot, you recognized us?'

She nods. Bumbling, trying to think straight, Tori asks, 'You called me Gloria. How could you know my name?'

'We named you long before you were born. Mother and I.'

The Woodleys add, 'Your romantic parents. Named their three children after movie stars. So cute.'

Harvey Woodley says with humor, 'Then he made us name all our horses after you. Insisting you would figure it out eventually and find us.'

'I knew you would recognize the clues sooner or later.' Grinning, Fred takes a photo from his wallet and hands it to her.

'This is me as a baby. What? How?'

Fred says, 'Your mama had our lawyer send it to me. It's all she had. The only photo Ida took of you. Unfortunately, my parents never took any.' He pauses. 'I'm so sorry, my parents treated you so badly.'

For a moment Tori thinks of the Steiners. Sad, now. Tori berates herself. Maybe if she'd been nicer to them, things would have been different. 'But how did you know?'

He reaches over and takes her hands for a few moments, smiling shyly at his daughter. 'Our lawyer kept me in touch all these years.'

Tori continues to glance around, searching, and worrying. Dix must be here, somewhere. Please, God, keep him away.

As Fred holds her closer, 'You must have so many questions.'

She leans into his chest. 'I do, Daddy, I do.'

'Then let me tell you.'

Forty-Seven
Fred's Story

The rain wouldn't stop. The sky had opened up and from it poured unending sheets of water. Nothing was going right. The plan had been to get into the bank, grab as much money as they could and get out of there. Fast. The bank customers, tellers, the bank manager, even the security guard wouldn't get down on the floor quick enough to suit edgy Dix who was demanding they get down. Now!

258

Fred was sorry he'd ever teamed up with these guys. Dockson and Hicks came along, without Dix telling him he had partners, too. His guys were too nervous, and Dix had a hair-trigger temper. Fred was afraid of how they might react in a situation that called for being icy calm.

Annoyed at the group's slowness to obey him, Dix lifted his shotgun, meant to just scare them, and started shooting wildly in the air. Which got Dockson yelling and Hicks starting to run for the door. People panicked, thinking he would kill them; were screaming, crying, and begging. Fred was terrified that Dix would shoot at them next.

Fred glanced quickly out the window where his pregnant wife sat waiting in their station wagon with the motor running. At that moment, Fred realized he'd just made the biggest mistake of his life. He should never have gone along with Chaz Dix's wild idea of bank robbing! More important, he should have insisted that Helen not come, she was too close to giving birth; but she'd argued they were in this together, and the plan needed her to be driving the car. Desperate as they were in their rush to get money, he now realized this was not the right answer to solving their financial problems. Dix and his two clowns were going to get them caught.

Finally Fred ran out the door behind Dix and the others. Getting soaked by the rain as he dumped the duffle bag through the open back window and climbed into the station wagon's passenger seat. The other three guys jumped into their jeep.

They were all to meet as soon as possible at their chosen rendezvous at an old barn in a wooded area of the valley and divvy up the loot.

As Helen drove, the rains worsened. Visibility was almost impossible. To her horror, she suddenly felt the baby kick too hard. She shuddered in fear. 'Not yet, baby, not now!' she said aloud.

Fred reacted in dismay. 'Is the baby coming?'

Helen didn't know, doesn't know, she can't think. Suddenly she's feeling as if something is happening in her body. 'Fred,' she screamed his name. 'You better drive!'

She pulled over to the nearest curb and they both got out, getting drenched, so they could change seats.

The water was nearly up to their knees!

The streets were flooding rapidly; the wind was whipping the water into frenzy. Helen almost lost her footing; Fred saved her with a desperate grab and pushed her into the passenger seat.

As Fred got behind the wheel, the car abruptly stalled. Helen's eyes widened in fear, her shock was so great that she couldn't even speak. She started to stutter. 'No, not now. Not here.'

It took him a while, the gears complaining, but finally Fred whooped wildly when he got the car re-started. The old station wagon skidded back onto the middle of the street as the water just kept rising.

Fred turned to Helen. They had to find a different way to get to the rendezvous point! But how? In terror, he realized Helen had her eyes closed, her hands circling her pregnant belly, as if trying to keep the baby from kicking its way out.

Fred made a decision. He spotted a small alley to his right and, whipping the wheel around, barely making the turn, suddenly losing his side mirror as it scraped against something, a mailbox, another car, he wasn't sure but it was gone. He could hardly see. The station wagon's windshield wipers were practically useless. Up ahead he suddenly spotted what looked like another wall of water flowing toward him!

There was only one way out.

Another turn. A blind turn to the left.

Fred had no choice. And suddenly Fred, Helen, their unborn baby, the bag of money he no longer cared about, and their crappy old station wagon were floating, carried by the force of the water down some kind of sluice, carried downward like some Disney ride from Hell, into the section known as The Wash, the thirty-foot-high concrete channel of the Los Angeles River, which cut through much of the city. A river wash that was always barren; now it was a flooded runoff trench from the storm, filling up with water. How did he end up in there?

They were going to die!

Both of them. And his baby.

His fault. His.

Helen suddenly yelled. 'Tree! Tree!' Fred could only stare, frozen, as the car smacked into the carcass of a tree which, felled by the wind and rain, had fallen into the Wash. The station wagon thunked into its thicket of dead and mangled branches, stopping the forward motion of the car. They were now in the middle of a raging river, caught in the arms of a broken tree.

It probably saved their lives.

The water pushed the tree, and shoved the car, higher up onto the banks of the Wash where they came to a stop. Helen pointed: 'There!'

Six feet from their car was a drainage tunnel. One they could reach on foot. A way out. Maybe.

Fred managed to open his car door, then to open Helen's door, and the two of them practically crawled to the dry lip of the drainage tunnel where, just like a prayer answered, they found a safe place to sit and catch their breath.

The tunnel was big enough so that they could stand in it without stooping. And both Fred and Helen could see that it led to a covered overpass, which towered over the flooded streets.

Fred held Helen close. Helen took his hand and placed it on her belly. The baby was now kicking mercilessly. 'Up a storm,' she joked, to lighten their situation. Then, followed by a sharp pain.

'We're okay now. Let me get to the car.'

'What are you doing?'

'I'm going to get the duffle bag out, spread a little of the cash in the car and push it downstream. That way, when they find it, they'll think all the money has been lost in the flood.'

'Be careful and hurry.'

When he got back minutes later, he found Helen hunched over, grabbing her belly harder.

Feeling pressured by time running out for them, he started to lift her up.

262

She cried out, 'No, stop! I can't move.'

Police sirens were heard coming close.

Helen gasped, 'You've got to get out of here. Now!'

'Help me lift you up.'

'No, not possible. No time.' Helen could hardly get the words out through the pain. 'You have to take the money and go!'

'I'm not leaving you here.'

'You have to. I can't be moved.'

The siren sounds grew ominous. Coming almost to them.

'They'll be here in minutes. I don't want them to catch you.'

'Helen, no!'

'They'll see a poor, pathetic pregnant woman. Alone. They'll feel sorry for me. I'll be all right. Get out. Get out of town. If something happens, whatever happens, you have to promise me, you'll escape. And never come back. When I can, I'll find you.' In her severe pain, she cried out, 'Promise me! For my sake and the sake of this baby who wants to come out now, get out of here. I swear, I'll be all right.'

'You promise some day we'll be together again.'

'I swear it. I'm begging you! Run and don't look back!'

With a last hopeless kiss, Fred climbed up and out into freedom. With a suitcase full of money.

His wife ended up in prison. Where their baby was born.

Forty-Eight

Meanwhile Back in the Stands

'. . . That's what happened. I left Helen, coward that I was. I hid out for days, not knowing what happened to her. Finally, I couldn't think of anything else to do, so I called my old friends in Florida . . .'

Lila finishes it, 'And we told him to get on the first flight to Fort Lauderdale.'

'And he's been with us since then.'

Harvey, 'The first three years he was here, we practically had to chain him to the bed, so wouldn't run back to Helen and also end up in prison.'

Lila, 'He was so ashamed of what he did.'

Fred, 'For good reason. I was stupid and reckless.'

Harvey, 'Very true, but what would be the point of your being imprisoned, too?'

Tori, 'But, Daddy . . . all these years, you lived so close, you never told Grandma Ida that you were here.'

Fred, 'I didn't trust her, I didn't dare. She deserted you and your mother. I never forgave her.'

Tori, 'You have no idea how she suffered, too.

How sorry she's been for leaving us all those years ago. We all suffered, and maybe it's time for forgiveness. I've forgiven her and you should, too.'

Fred looks at her lovingly. 'Then I shall follow my smart girl's advice.'

She looks behind her, anxiously searching. 'Why didn't you tell the police about Dix and your other partners?'

Fred. 'Supposing those three were the ones who landed in prison and *we'd* both escaped. We would expect them not to rat on us. We had to do the same.'

Fearfully, Tori thinks of those partners so close, with murder on their minds. If the opposite had happened, Dix would not have done the same for them. Dix would have turned them in to save himself.

'Your poor mother, still in there, but maybe not for much longer. When she gets out we'll be together again. Please, God.'

'Really? Is that possible?'

'I'll know more very soon. Our lawyer . . . But it hasn't happened just yet.'

Harvey Woodley comments, 'It all has to do with your father returning the bank's money years ago.'

Fred adds, 'Helen knew you would be coming. She knew you'd figure out where I was. And by God, here you are!' He reaches over and takes her hands for a few moments, smiling shyly at his daughter. They exchange small kisses.

Suddenly Tori stiffens. She was afraid this would happen.

She grabs at her father's arms, pulling at him. 'What is it? What's wrong?' All three glance at her worriedly.

Tori. 'You don't understand. They're here! Dix, Hicks and Dockson.'

Fred is startled, trying to understand what she is saying. 'You know them? My partners?'

'They used me to find you. They followed me from California. Dix wants the money and revenge. I think he intends to kill you!'

Harvey Woodley, 'Here? Right now?'

'We've got to hide!' Tori insists, as she keeps pulling at them with growing fright.

Tori found them! I'm a good Spotter, after all! I can observe her far down below me, excitedly talking to a well-dressed, handsome middle-aged couple and their partner. She did it – she located the Woodleys and surely her father!

But I can see what they don't see. Dix and his guys are in their section, racing up the steps to reach her. They have found Tori and now realize they've found Fred Steiner.

Though Hicks is lagging behind, a man fighting his demons.

Tori sees them. She's trying to get the three of them to run in another direction!

Morrie and Jack are far away.

I panic. I jump up, but what can I do? I can't get to them. But, even if I reached them, how could I help? These guys have guns.

I remember the borrowed cell phone. I must alert Morrie and Jack. With shaking hands I dial Jack's number. I stop short. I can't remember it.

266

The phone numbers I once memorized are no longer necessary; the speed dial remembers for me. So one tends to forget. Which is happening to me now. But, more to the point, this isn't my phone. It won't be my caller ID. That's a bigger problem. Jack won't know it's me calling. I dial twice, the numbers jumbled. I calm myself down and think, until I have the digits in the right order.

This time I get through to Jack's cell. And it just keeps ringing. I was afraid this would happen. He's too busy with Morrie to answer a phone number he doesn't recognize. I hang up and dial again. Let it ring twice. Hang up and dial again. Over and over again, I repeat. It works. This gets his attention. He answers, curious, 'Hello. Who is this?'

I practically whimper. 'Dix is catching up to Tori and her dad.'

Jack is quick. He knows it's me and he hears my fear and doesn't waste time with small talk. 'Where?'

How can I tell him? He won't understand what I know, thanks to my racetrack-lover Dad. 'Jack, they're halfway between the sixteenth pole and the finish line! Ask someone!'

Jack doesn't know what that means, but he recalls where he left me. I see him waving to me and I jump up and point down and across the seats, and point some more, hoping he gets what I'm desperately signaling.

And he does. Because I see him grab Morrie's arm. Morrie signals to his men to stretch out and follow. They run zigzag through the stands;

267

bettors are watching them with interest, sensing some drama taking place. They are torn between their curiosity – why are cops running about and what's going on? – and following the next race, hoping for winners.

I continue to indicate, trying to hold back the dread I feel. Will they get there in time?

The horses are lined up at the starting gate for the next half-mile stretch, waiting for the signal to take off. The race in the stands competes with the race on the track – almost funny to watch, in an unfunny situation. Like a Keystone Kops silent film.

Dix sees the cops coming his way. He moves faster.

Tori becomes aware of the distracted shuffling of people around them. She turns to see what they see. The moment she spots Dix, she pushes at her threesome and points. 'Run faster!' she shouts. 'They're closing in on us!' They do the best they can, twisting their way up through the miles of people in their seats.

Dix is breathing hard. They're fifty feet away. Dix smiles, smelling success.

Hicks says, 'You're too far off, you'll never get them.'

'Shut up.' Dix doesn't want to hear from him. He aims his gun, ready to take a shot at Fred. 'I'm gonna kill the bastard!'

Hicks laughs, 'Now seventy-five feet. You're losing ground.'

Dix stares at his running target. When he looks around, he sees the cops are coming at him from all sides. They're gaining on him! He finally realizes he's outnumbered. With a frustrated last glance at his prey, he and Dockson reverse pattern and rush back down the steps, trying to evade the cops getting closer to them.

Hicks merely plants himself on the nearest seat to await his fate, head in his hands. He's done.

Tori shouts to Morrie and Jack. 'Hurry! Catch them!'

The cops reverse their order.

Dix and Dockson fight their way back down the steps, arriving where the scattered bettors stand, leaning on the rail. The racetrack aficionados turn, seeing a confusing sight. The cops are almost where they are. And so are three men trying to avoid them.

There is nowhere for Dix to turn. Except to try to escape through the infield. And the only way to get there . . .

. . . Dix, pushing people out of his way, leaps over the fence and onto the racetrack. Dockson stops a moment, then, fearfully, he jumps over as well. People scream, horrified. What on earth is going on? Don't those guys know that there are ten heavyweight horses that will be bearing down on them any minute?

The starting buzzer is heard. The horses, with their jockeys holding tight to the reins, are coming their way, full speed; jockeys using their whips, urging their mounts to run faster, kicking up sand and dust. Making the turn in record time.

With inches to spare from the hooves of the thundering herd, Dix takes a desperate leap over the infield fence, where racetrack staffers watch in horror. Dockson tries to escape the onrush of

269

horses' hooves and is too late. He is knocked down by the first two horses, racing neck and neck, edging their way toward win and place. People in the stands scream some more.

The diehards cheer as their Panorama Stables horse goes past the finish line. However, there's another horse with him, neck and neck.

Tori, Fred and the Woodleys watch the capture, fascinated. But, thank God, Tori is relieved. Her daddy is safe. They are all safe.

Dix lands over the infield fence, head first into a bougainvillea trellis, only to peer up to see a gun in his face and the smiling cop holding it.

Dockson never makes it to the infield fence; he ends up with a broken leg. No horses were injured.

It's a photo finish. The winner is Morning Glory! Pays $9.20 to win.

Izzy does get to speak to his son, once they are both back at police headquarters. Izzy hopes to share a cell. His request is denied.

Dix rudely ignores his father. 'Who the hell are you, anyway?'

'If you came home more often, you'd know. I'm you're father, Chaz, my boy. By the way, did you like living in my house? And where's my Edsel?'

Dix walks away, totally uninterested. 'Get lost.'

Izzy, a closet intellectual and basically upbeat guy, chooses a Shakespearean quotation to make himself feel better. He shrugs his shoulders and quotes, 'How sharper than a serpent's tooth it is to have a thankless child.'

'Right on, King Lear,' he says as he's shown back to his cell. The guard couldn't care less as he turns the key in the lock.

Forty-Nine
Long Distance

The girls are gathered in my tiny kitchen where my phone lives. They sit crowded at my equally small kitchen table, chomping away on bagels slathered with lox, cream cheese, tomatoes and red onion. With coleslaw on the side. Hold the capers. Decaf coffee 'to wash it down with.' Bella insists the food will give them strength.

Strength for what? To listen? She and Sophie have been quite odd lately.

I stand near the window, waiting. I repeat the rules I set down. 'No talking when we talk or I won't be able to hear what she's saying.' It's been arranged. Ida will call promptly at noon; nine a.m. her time in LA. Tori, Ida and Fred have been gone for two weeks. We are all excited, waiting to hear the news from the other coast.

Everyone stares at the clock on my wall, watching the second hand going round.

The phone rings on the dot. As planned, I answer on the speaker-phone, so they will hear everything as well. Saves me having to repeat myself.

The phone call:

Me, 'Hello Ida.'

Ida, 'Hello, everybody. Hello, Gladdy. Hello, Evvie. Hello Sophie and Bella.' (One unit, twins as usual.) This is the sound of a happy person. Grumpy Ida is no more?

The girls shout at the phone, 'Hello. Hello. Hello.'

Me (making small talk), How's the weather out there?

Sophie, 'Who cares about the weather? It's sunny there. It's sunny here. It's sunny everywhere. So, what happened with Tori?'

Me, 'Sophie, I said keep out!'

Sophie, 'Well you're too slow getting to the point.'

Evvie, 'Sophie. Shut up. Let Gladdy do it her way.'

Me (glaring at Sophie), 'So, Ida, what's going on?'

Ida, 'It's been incredible. Tori and I and Fred went to visit Helen in prison.'

Bella (confused as usual), 'You mean they went to see him go to jail, too?

Me, 'Bella. Shh . . . listen.'

Ida, 'It's amazing and everything's happened so fast. When Fred escaped and arrived at Fort Lauderdale and met up with the Woodleys, they got him to a great lawyer who worked along with his LA lawyer, with orders not to reveal who he is or where he is. Something to do with lawyer-client privilege about privacy. Between them, Fred sent back all the stolen money.'

Bella, 'Fred didn't drown? The money didn't get wet. He didn't spend it?'

Evvie comforts her. 'We'll explain it to you later. Okay? Get some more coffee and relax.'

Bella gratefully heads for the coffee pot.

Sophie, 'He sent the money back?'

Me (to Sophie), 'Can't you wait a minute? Must you always jump the gun? I was getting there.'

Sophie and Bella shake hands. They giggle. Evvie and I exchange a glance. Those two are weird. If I didn't know better, I'd think they're on drugs. Nah, not them . . .

Ida, 'The bank didn't want to press charges, relieved that they got their money back. And the DA didn't intend to press charges either, because it had passed the statute of limitations. I don't really understand, but it's good news, isn't it?'

Sophie and Bella yell out in unison. 'Great!'

Bella is about to refill her coffee and drops the ceramic cup on the floor. Crash. Loud whispering follows – Bella in an argument with Sophie. I shake my fist at them to be quiet. Sophie is warning Bella about something purple that she ate? Huh? I try to ignore them.

Me, 'Ida, that's wonderful news.'

Ida, 'More legal stuff. I don't understand any of it, but here's the scoop. Dix and guys didn't get arrested for the bank job, but they couldn't escape the kidnapping charge. Hicks made a deal with the cops, telling them all about the kidnapping, so he wouldn't have to go to jail, or maybe he'll just serve a short term, I don't know. But he's all right, because he turned something called state's evidence on Dix and Dockson. There's no statute of limitation for kidnapping; Dix will be in prison forever. Dix is toast.

'And more great news, their lawyer who has

273

been working on it for years is close to getting Helen out of prison soon.'

Evvie cheers.

Ida. 'That's when we went to prison to visit Helen to tell her the big news. And you should have seen their faces – Fred and Helen. Like fifteen years never happened. They weren't allowed to touch, but they were sending air-kisses like crazy. Tori and I were eating it up. A reunion, just like in the movies.'

Bella, the sentimental one. 'Ahh, that's sweet.'

Sophie (furious), 'He dumps her, nine months pregnant, and runs away with all the stolen money. She rots in jail and he becomes a million-aire and Helen forgives him!'

Evvie, 'They made that pact.'

Bella yells, 'Hooray!'

Me, 'Bella, don't step on the glass.' Bella is still on her knees searching the floor.

Sophie goes to help her pick up the coffee-cup pieces. They are making so much noise in that tiny space, that I have to hold my ear to the phone in order to listen to Ida.

Ida, 'And you know what else is wonderful? I've met with Shirley and Marilyn, my beautiful granddaughters.'

I can hear her telling me this, all choked up. 'They are such lovely women. And I got to hold my adorable great-grandchildren. And, hope-fully, my daughter will be released soon. Everything is good. What? Hold on. Gladdy, I'm being called. Gotta go. We're all going out to someplace special, Solly's deli for breakfast. Love to all and Tori says hi.'

She hangs up and so do I.

Wow! Silence for a few moments as we respond emotionally to all that news.

The door opens and Jack enters, carrying today's newspaper. He announces, 'Have you seen what's going on outside?'

'No, we've been on the phone with Ida. I can't wait to fill you in.'

Evvie asks Jack, looking toward the door, 'What's happening?'

'Selma is banging on Sophie's door, yelling something about suing her next-door neighbor for a broken wall.'

Sophie takes Bella's hand and they skulk toward the door. They offer up no information as they tiptoe out. But they look anxious.

I wonder what that's about. 'Jack, sit down. Want lunch?'

Evvie says, 'Gladdy, did you hear the last thing Ida said?'

'Goodbye?'

'No, after that. She said, 'Gloria says hi.'

I think on it. 'Gloria? Not Tori? Hmmm. That's a really good omen. I think.'

Evvie adds, 'A happy ending.'

Jack turns to me. He's at the open refrigerator. 'Who ate all the bagels? A guy can starve around this place.'

Evvie and I laugh. Life is back to normal.

Acknowledgements

To my best fans; my sister, Judy and my grand-daughter Alison and my good friends.

To Nancy Yost and all the gang at NY Literary.

To my critique gang: For their appreciation for the Gladdy books: Peggy Lucke, the two Lambs-Bette and JJ, Nicola Trwst, Gwen Kauffman, Judith Yamamoto and Ken Gwin.

To Camille Minichino, Kelli Stanley and Priscilla Royal who read all the Gladdy books. Wonderful friends and writers that they are.

And to the many wonderful fans who keep writing; asking when the next Gladdy books will be available. Thank you for your loyalty. And here they are.

And thanks to my faithful special readers Sandy Carp and Lois Leonard.